The Holly-Tree Inn

The Holly-Tree Inn

Charles Dickens

with
Wilkie Collins
William Howitt
Adelaide Anne Procter
Harriet Parr

Edited by
Melisa Klimaszewski

ET REMOTISSIMA PROPE

Hesperus Classics

Hesperus Classics
Published by Hesperus Press Limited
4 Rickett Street, London SW6 1RU
www.hesperuspress.com

First published in *Household Words* in 1855
First published by Hesperus Press Limited, 2009

This edition edited by Melisa Klimaszewski
Introduction and notes © Melisa Klimaszewski, 2009

Designed and typeset by Fraser Muggeridge studio
Printed in Jordan by Jordan National Press

ISBN: 978-1-84391-196-8

CONTENTS

INTRODUCTION

A bashful man in a cavernous room contemplating drapery that resembles 'gigantic worms', the first narrator of *The Holly-Tree Inn* presents us with thoughts that feel rather rambling. Reminiscing about the various inns he has visited seems like a fine idea to help him pass time during a snowstorm, but one gets the sense that the speaker does not remain in complete control of where the anecdotes take him. Charley, or 'The Guest', experiences the challenges of narrative compilation in a manner that resembles the ordeals his creator, Charles Dickens, faced but did not necessarily anticipate when he conceived of the narrative frame for this Christmas number.

The Holly-Tree Inn was the sixth special Christmas issue, or number, of Dickens' journal *Household Words*, but only the second for which he used a theme to construct a complete narrative frame story. *The Seven Poor Travellers*, 1854's Christmas number, moved beyond the loose frame concept of *A Round of Stories by the Christmas Fire* (1852) and *Another Round of Stories by the Christmas Fire* (1853) by describing all of the narrators at a charity house and by linking the first and last stories to construct an explicit frame. Building upon those results, *The Holly-Tree Inn* continues to use travel and lodging for its organising theme. In early October of 1855, Dickens composed instructions to prospective contributors that make clear his narrative aims:

> *Both for the sake of variety between this No. and the previous Christmas numbers, and also for the preservation of the idea, it is necessary that the stories should not be in the first person, but should be turned as if this traveller were recording them. … the person to whom the story belongs may be described,*

*if necessary, as pretty or ugly – of such an age – of such a bringing up – and what is related about him or her may have happened at that Inn, or at another Inn, or at no Inn; and may belong to that person's present condition in life, or to some previous condition in life – and not only to himself or herself, but (if necessary) to other persons encountered in life.**

Such open-ended instructions would seem to invite just about any type of story, but Dickens was less than thrilled with the initial contributions. Writing to his sub-editor, W.H. Wills, Dickens called one of the rejected stories 'unmitigated, bawdy Rot' and complained, 'The way in which they *don't* fit into that elaborately described plan, so simple in itself, amazes me.'† Since the 'elaborately described plan' included no guidelines pertaining to topic, the problems Dickens encountered may have stemmed more from his own lack of precise instruction rather than from the stories not actually fitting into the frame. One of his specific complaints, for instance, was that too many of the initial contributions were about criminals, yet his practice was not to suggest plots for contributors, which always left open the possibility that their stories could be similar.

Dickens was particularly invested in making the sure the finalised set of stories was a good one because his name was the only one to appear in print on the Christmas issue. Writers for all issues of *Household Words* agreed to sacrifice bylines in order for the journal to attempt to maintain a unified and

* *The Pilgrim Edition of the Letters of Charles Dickens,* vol. 7 (Oxford: 1993) pp. 713–4

† 24th November 1855, *Pilgrim Letters* vol. 7, p. 753

‡ 12th December 1855, *Pilgrim Letters* vol. 7, p. 762

distinctive voice, which was not unusual in the Victorian periodical press. The Christmas numbers were no exception. Their title pages stated that they were 'Conducted by Charles Dickens' with no other authors' names appearing in the contents list. The conductor metaphor acknowledges without naming the presence of other creative talent. General readers would be familiar with such editorial practices, which left them unable to discern exactly who wrote each individual piece. While Dickens could always disclaim authorship of stories the public did not appreciate, the critical tendency among readers and reviewers was not only to give Dickens credit for what was good in the Christmas numbers but also to blame him for anything deemed displeasing.

Ultimately, all but two of the contributions Dickens selected for the number came from writers who had written for previous Christmas collections. Only Harriet Parr and William Howitt were new Christmas number contributors, but each had written for regular *Household Words* issues. Still, even Wilkie Collins, a close friend of Dickens who would become his closest collaborator, wrote a story that Dickens asked him to revise. In thanking Collins for the revision, Dickens also explained:

> *The botheration of that No. has been prodigious. The general matter was so disappointing and so impossible to be fitted together or got into the frame, that after I had done the Guest and the Bill and thought myself free for* Little Dorrit *again, I had to go back once more (feeling the thing too weak), and do the Boots. Look at said Boots, – because I think its* [sic] *an odd idea, and gets something of the effect of a Fairy Story out of the most unlikely materials.*‡

'The Boots' produces a remarkable effect indeed, with the unforgettable Cobbs relating a touching story of precocious children determined to elope. The tale was such a favourite, and Cobbs such an inviting voice to perform, that Dickens included 'The Boots at the Holly-Tree Inn' in his later public readings. The rest of the number testifies to the success of Dickens' efforts to craft a pleasing issue with a variety of subjects.

'The Guest', more harassed than charmed by elements associated with idyllic Christmases – a snowstorm, 'Auld Lang Syne', refuge at a warm inn – begins the number with a dejected tone that nevertheless peaks readers' curiosity. Insightfully noting that, before discovering the charms of a new place, many travellers arrive at a destination only to 'immediately want to go away from it', this first narrator's affability ensures that his readers' initial response to the Holly-Tree Inn will be anything but repugnance. In spite of beheadings, unburied corpses, and a 'suicide bed', we want to read more.

The thematic resonances between the frame and the inset stories make the Holly-Tree Inn a place full of symbolic value in the narrator's individual family but also in the broader national vision of mid-nineteenth-century Englishness, which insisted upon and celebrated the capacity of an English Holly-Tree to be spread 'all over the world'. The Guest in his final remarks, the Landlord, and the Poor Pensioner demonstrate the difficulty of balancing the rewards and the perils of the colonial endeavours whose existence testified to the hubris of the colonial project itself. The Tattenhall family in William Howitt's story, related by the landlord, certainly share the guest's desire to immediately flee their destination when they arrive in Australia, a journey for which the children prepared by reading about other colonial travellers in South Africa.

Howitt's piece later appeared as 'The Melbourne Merchant' in his *Tallangetta, the Squatters Home. A Story of Australian Life* (1857). In Harriet Parr's story, the poor pensioner's time in India with her husband leads to far less pleasing results than the Tattenhalls' stay in Australia. Not only do Hester's experiences of 'camp life' threaten traditional constructions of English femininity by teaching her profanities 'which she used with vigorous truth when her wrath was excited', the family life that she constructs once she returns to England results in dysfunction, jealousy, and devastating accusations of murder.

The looming threat of murder also hangs over 'The Ostler', Wilkie Collins' Gothic tale that links dreams and premonitions of murder to a protagonist plagued by bad luck. Most haunting is the ostler's continued fear of his potential murderess and his inability to resolve the fear with purposeful action. Interestingly, when Collins later performed public readings like the ones Dickens had innovated and in which he included 'The Boots', Collins revised 'The Ostler' and performed it as 'The Dream Woman'. Adelaide Ann Procter approaches death from a different perspective in the short verse recounted by the barmaid, which treats the innocence of youthful romance with a poignancy that echoes 'The Boots'. Maurice's longing from afar and the progression of naive children into a more jaded adulthood links his experiences across class boundaries to little Harry Walmers in 'The Boots'.

In addition to thematic resonances between the stories, there are moments where the narrators' voices get confused, which points to the challenges created by the type of frame story Dickens devised. For all of Dickens' worry about the stories fitting together, the short moments of awkwardness between stories also point toward the most interesting moments of collaboration.

In 'The Ostler', for instance, it sometimes becomes difficult to keep track of who is telling the story, particularly because the ostler does not actually narrate his tale to the guest. The landlord of the Holly-Tree Inn provides the tale about the ostler, which involves the ostler's interactions with a different landlord. The landlord of the Holly-Tree Inn, then, actually relates two tales in the collection, 'The Ostler' and 'The Landlord', written by two different authors. That Dickens probably wrote some of the connecting passages makes it even harder to distinguish each authorial voice with precision.

For a story with a frame, such as *The Holly-Tree Inn*, Dickens would sometimes write or edit the passages linking one story to another, but since the manuscripts and proof pages have not survived, we do not know exactly who wrote which sentences in the passages between stories. It seems likely that Dickens wrote the lead-in for Procter's verse, in which case he took care to gesture, somewhat awkwardly, toward the fact that he did not compose the verse itself. Although the guest records what the barmaid related, he also states, 'She told me a tale of that country which went so pleasantly to the music of her voice, that I ought rather to say it turned itself into verse, than was turned into verse by me.' Spontaneous transformation into verse does not exactly acknowledge Procter's creative process, but it does distance the guest from taking any credit for the poem's aesthetic merit. In the instructions he issued to potential contributors, Dickens was confident in the narrative voices of multiple contributors all coming together into the single voice of the stranded traveller. The degree to which the voices merge successfully may vary throughout the number, but ultimately, his audience was pleased with the result.

Whether or not *The Holly-Tree Inn*'s first readers recognised its original in the George and New Inn, located in Yorkshire, and whether or not the other inns the guest remembers felt familiar to them, they enjoyed the collection of stories just as much as, if not more than, previous Christmas numbers. Sales were strong, and Dickens was relieved to have pleased the holiday audience to which he felt responsible each December.

– *Melisa Klimaszewski, 2009*

The Holly-Tree Inn

Being the Extra Christmas Number
Of Household Words

Conducted By Charles Dickens

Containing The Amount Of
One Number And A Half

Christmas, 1855

THE GUEST
[by Charles Dickens]

I have kept one secret in the course of my life. I am a bashful man. Nobody would suppose it, nobody ever does suppose it, nobody ever did suppose it. But, I am naturally a bashful man. This is the secret which I have never breathed until now.

I might greatly move the reader, by some account of the innumerable places I have not been to, the innumerable people I have not called upon or received, the innumerable social evasions I have been guilty of, solely because I am by original constitution and character, a bashful man. But, I will leave the reader unmoved, and proceed with the object before me.

That object is, to give a plain account of my travels and discoveries in the Holly-Tree Inn; in which place of good entertainment for man and beast, I was once snowed up.

It happened in the memorable year when I parted forever from Angela Leath whom I was shortly to have married, on making the discovery that she preferred my bosom friend. From our schooldays I had freely admitted Edwin, in my own mind, to be far superior to myself, and, though I was grievously wounded at heart, I felt the preference to be natural, and tried to forgive them both. It was under these circumstances that I resolved to go to America – on my way to the Devil.

Communicating my discovery neither to Angela nor to Edwin, but resolving to write each of them an affecting letter conveying my blessing and forgiveness, which the steam-tender for shore should carry to the post when I myself should be bound for the New World, far beyond recall; – I say, locking up my grief in my own breast, and consoling myself as I could, with the prospect of being generous, I quietly left all I held dear, and started on the desolate journey I have mentioned.

The dead wintertime was in full dreariness when I left my chambers forever, at five o'clock in the morning. I had shaved by candlelight, of course, and was miserably cold, and experienced that general all-pervading sensation of getting up to be hanged, which I have usually found inseparable from untimely rising under such circumstances.

How well I remember the forlorn aspect of Fleet Street when I came out of the Temple![1] The street lamps flickering in the gusty north-east wind, as if the very gas were contorted with cold; the white-topped houses; the bleak, star-lighted sky; the market people and other early stragglers, trotting, to circulate their almost frozen blood; the hospitable light and warmth of the few coffee shops and public houses that were open for such customers; the hard, dry, frosty rime with which the air was charged (the wind had already beaten it into every crevice), and which lashed my face like a steel whip.[2]

It wanted nine days to the end of the month, and end of the year. The post office packet for the United States was to depart from Liverpool, weather permitting, on the first of the ensuing month, and I had the intervening time on my hands. I had taken this into consideration, and had resolved to make a visit to a certain spot (which I need not name), on the further borders of Yorkshire. It was endeared to me by my having first seen Angela at a farmhouse in that place, and my melancholy was gratified by the idea of taking a wintry leave of it before my expatriation. I ought to explain, that to avoid being sought out before my resolution should have been rendered irrevocable by being carried into full effect, I had written to Angela overnight, in my usual manner, lamenting that urgent business – of which she should know all particulars by-and-by – took me unexpectedly away from her for a week or ten days.

There was no Northern Railway[3] at that time, and in its place there were stagecoaches: which I occasionally find myself, in common with some other people, affecting to lament now, but which everybody dreaded as a very serious penance then. I had secured the box-seat[4] on the fastest of these, and my business in Fleet Street was, to get into a cab with my portmanteau, so to make the best of my way to the Peacock at Islington, where I was to join this coach. But, when one of our Temple watchmen who carried my portmanteau into Fleet Street for me, told me about the huge blocks of ice that had for some days past been floating in the river, having closed up in the night and made a walk from the Temple Gardens over to the Surrey shore, I began to ask myself the question, Whether the box-seat would not be likely to put a sudden and a frosty end to my unhappiness? I was heartbroken, it is true, and yet I was not quite so far gone as to wish to be frozen to death.

When I got up to the Peacock – where I found everybody drinking hot purl, in self-preservation – I asked, if there were an inside seat to spare?[5] I then discovered that, inside or out, I was the only passenger. This gave me a still livelier idea of the great inclemency of the weather, since that coach always loaded particularly well. However, I took a little purl (which I found uncommonly good), and got into the coach. When I was seated, they built me up with straw to the waist, and, conscious of making a rather ridiculous appearance, I began my journey.

It was still dark when we left the Peacock. For a little while, pale uncertain ghosts of houses and trees appeared and vanished, and then it was hard, black, frozen day. People were lighting their fires; smoke was mounting straight up, high into the rarified air; and we were rattling for Highgate Archway[6] over the hardest ground I have ever heard the ring of iron shoes on. As we got into the country, everything seemed to have grown old and grey. The roads, the trees, thatched roofs of cottages and homesteads, the ricks in farmers' yards. Outdoor work was abandoned, horse troughs at roadside Inns were frozen hard, no stragglers lounged about, doors were close shut, little turnpike-houses had blazing fires inside, and children (even turnpike-people have children, and seem to like them), rubbed the frost from the little panes of glass with their chubby arms, that their bright eyes might catch a glimpse of the solitary coach going by. I don't know when the snow began to set in; but, I know that we were changing horses somewhere when I heard the guard remark, 'That the old lady up in the sky was picking her geese pretty hard today.' Then, indeed, I found the white down falling fast and thick.

The lonely day wore on, and I dozed it out as a lonely traveller does. I was warm and valiant after eating and drinking, particularly after dinner; cold and depressed at all other times. I was always bewildered as to time and place, and always more or less out of my senses. The coach and horses seemed to execute in chorus, Auld Lang Syne,[7] without a moment's intermission. They kept the time and tune with the greatest regularity, and rose into the swell at the beginning of the Refrain, with a precision that worried me to death. While we changed horses, the guard and coachman went stumping up and down the road, printing off their shoes in the snow, and pouring so much liquid consolation into themselves without being any the worse for it, that I began to confound them, as it darkened again, with two great white casks standing on end. Our horses tumbled down in solitary places, and we got them up – which was the pleasantest variety *I* had, for it warmed me. And it snowed and snowed, and still it snowed, and never left off snowing. All night long, we went on in this manner. Thus, we came round the clock, upon the Great North Road,[8] to the performance of Auld Lang Syne by day again. And it snowed and snowed, and still it snowed, and never left off snowing.

I forget now, where we were at noon on the second day, and where we ought to have been; but, I know that we were scores of miles behindhand, and that our case was growing worse every hour. The drift was becoming prodigiously deep; landmarks were getting snowed out; the road and the fields were all one; instead of having fences and hedgerows to guide us, we went crunching on, over an unbroken surface of ghastly white that might sink beneath us at any moment and drop us down a whole hillside. Still, the coachman and guard – who kept together on the box, always in council, and looking well about them – made out the track with astonishing sagacity.

When we came in sight of a town, it looked, to my fancy, like a large drawing on a slate, with abundance of slate-pencil expended on the churches and houses where the snow lay thickest. When we came within a town, and found the church clocks all stopped, the dial-faces choked with snow, and the Inn signs blotted out, it seemed as if the whole place were overgrown with white moss. As to the coach, it was a mere snowball; similarly, the men and boys who ran along beside us to the town's end, turning our clogged wheels and encouraging our horses, were men and boys of snow; and the bleak wild solitude to which they at last dismissed us, was a snowy Saharah. One would have thought this enough; notwithstanding which, I pledge my word that it snowed and snowed, and still it snowed, and never left off snowing.

We performed Auld Lang Syne the whole day; seeing nothing, out of towns and villages, but the track of stoats, hares, and foxes, and sometimes of birds. At nine o'clock at night, on a Yorkshire moor, a cheerful burst from our horn, and a welcome sound of talking, with a glimmering and moving about of lanterns, roused me from my drowsy state. I found that we were going to change.

They helped me out, and I said to a waiter, whose bare head became as white as King Lear's in a single minute; 'What Inn is this?'

'The Holly-Tree, sir,' said he.

'Upon my word, I believe,' said I, apologetically to the guard and coachman, 'that I must stop here.'

Now, the landlord, and the landlady, and the ostler, and the postboy, and all the stable authorities, had already asked the coachman, to the wide-eyed interest of all the rest of the establishment, if he meant to go on? The coachman had already replied, 'Yes, he'd take her through it' – meaning by Her, the coach – 'if so be as George would stand by him.' George was the guard, and he had already sworn that he *would* stand by him. So, the helpers were already getting the horses out.

My declaring myself beaten, after this parley, was not an announcement without preparation. Indeed, but for the way to the announcement being smoothed by the parley, I more than doubt whether, as an innately bashful man, I should have had the confidence to make it. As it was, it received the approval, even of the guard and coachman. Therefore, with many confirmations of my inclining, and many remarks from one bystander to another, that the gentleman could go for'ard by the mail tomorrow, whereas tonight he would only be froze, and where was the good of a gentleman being froze – ah, let alone buried alive (which latter clause was added by a humorous helper as a joke at my expense, and was extremely well received), I saw my portmanteau got out stiff, like a frozen body; did the handsome thing by the guard and coachman; wished them good night and a prosperous journey; and, a little ashamed of myself after all, for leaving them to fight it out alone, followed the landlord, landlady, and waiter of the Holly-Tree, upstairs.

I thought I had never seen such a large room as that into which they showed me. It had five windows, with dark red curtains that would have absorbed the light of a general illumination; and there were complications of drapery at the top of the curtains, that went wandering about the wall in a most extraordinary manner. I asked for a smaller room, and they told me there was no smaller room. They could screen me in, however, the landlord said. They brought a great old japanned[9] screen, with natives (Japanese, I suppose), engaged in a variety of idiotic pursuits all over it; and left me, roasting whole before an immense fire.

My bedroom was some quarter of a mile off, up a great staircase, at the end of a long gallery; and nobody knows what a misery this is to a bashful man who would rather not meet people on the stairs. It was the grimmest room I have ever had the nightmare in; and all the furniture, from the four posts of the bed to the two old silver candlesticks, was tall, high-shouldered, and spindle-waisted. Below, in my sitting room, if I looked round my screen, the wind rushed at me like a mad bull; if I stuck to my armchair, the fire scorched me to the colour of a new brick. The chimneypiece was very high, and there was a bad glass – what I may call a wavy glass – above it, which, when I stood up, just showed me my anterior phrenological[10] developments – and these never look well, in any subject, cut short off at the eyebrow. If I stood with my back to the fire, a gloomy vault of darkness above and beyond the screen insisted on being looked at; and, in its dim remoteness, the drapery of the ten curtains of the five windows went twisting and creeping about, like a nest of gigantic worms.

I suppose that what I observe in myself must be observed by some other men of similar character in *themselves*; therefore I am emboldened to mention, that when I travel, I never arrive at a place but I immediately want to go away from it. Before I had finished my supper of broiled fowl and mulled port, I had impressed upon the waiter in detail, my arrangements for departure in the morning. Breakfast and bill at eight. Fly at nine. Two horses, or, if needful, even four.

Tired though I was, the night appeared about a week long. In cases of nightmare, I thought of Angela, and felt more depressed than ever by the reflection that I was on the shortest road to Gretna Green.[11] What had *I* to do at Gretna Green? I was not going *that* way to the devil, but by the American route, I remarked, in my bitterness.

In the morning I found that it was snowing still, that it had snowed all night, and that I was snowed up. Nothing could get out of that spot on the moor, or could come at it, until the road had been cut out by laborers from the market town. When they might cut their way to the Holly-Tree, nobody could tell me.

It was now Christmas Eve. I should have had a dismal Christmas time of it anywhere, and, consequently, that did not so much matter; still, being snowed up, was, like dying of frost, a thing I had not bargained for. I felt very lonely. Yet I could no more have proposed to the landlord and landlady to admit me to their society (though I should have liked it very much), than I could have asked them to present me with a piece of plate. Here my great secret, the real bashfulness of my character, is to be observed. Like most bashful men, I judge of other people as if they were bashful too. Besides being far too shame-faced to make the proposal myself, I really had a delicate misgiving that it would be in the last degree disconcerting to them.

Trying to settle down, therefore, in my solitude, I first of all asked what books there were in the house? The waiter brought me a Book of Roads, two or three old Newspapers, a little Song-book terminating in a collection of Toasts and Sentiments, a little Jest-book, an odd volume of *Peregrine Pickle*, and the *Sentimental Journey*.[12] I knew every word of the two last already, but I read them through again: then tried to hum all the songs (Auld Lang Syne was among them); went entirely through the jokes – in which I found a fund of melancholy adapted to my state of mind; proposed all the toasts, enunciated all the sentiments, and mastered the papers. The latter had nothing in them but Stock advertisements, a meeting about a count rate, and a highway robbery. As I am a greedy reader, I could not make this supply hold out until night; it was exhausted by teatime. Being then entirely cast upon my own resources, I got through an hour in considering what to do next. Ultimately, it came into my head (from which I was anxious by any means to exclude Angela and Edwin), that I would endeavour to recall my experience of Inns, and would try how long it lasted me. I stirred the fire, moved my chair a little to one side of the screen – not daring to go far, for I knew the wind was waiting to make a rush at me – I could hear it growling – and began.

My first impressions of an Inn, dated from the Nursery; consequently, I went back to the Nursery for a starting point, and found myself at the knee of a sallow woman with a fishy eye, an aquiline nose, and a green gown, whose speciality was a dismal narrative of a landlord by the roadside, whose visitors unaccountably disappeared for many years, until it was discovered that the pursuit of his life had been to convert them into pies. For the better devotion of himself to this branch of industry, he had constructed a secret door behind the head of the bed; and when the visitor (oppressed with pie), had fallen asleep, this wicked landlord would look softly in with a lamp in one hand and a knife in the other, would cut his throat, and would make him into pies; for which purpose he had coppers underneath a trapdoor, always boiling; and rolled out his pastry in the dead of the night. Yet even he was not insensible to the stings of conscience, for he never went to sleep without being heard to mutter, 'Too much pepper!' – which was eventually the cause of his being brought to justice. I had no sooner disposed of this criminal than there started up another, of the same period, whose profession was, originally, housebreaking; in the pursuit of which art he had had his right ear chopped off one night as he was burglariously getting in at a window, by a brave and lovely servant maid (whom the aquiline-nosed woman, though not at all answering the description, always mysteriously implied to be herself). After several years, this brave and lovely servant maid was married to the landlord of a country Inn: which landlord had this remarkable characteristic, that he always wore a silk nightcap, and never would, on any consideration, take it off. At last, one night, when he was fast asleep, the brave and lovely woman lifted up his silk nightcap on the right side, and found that he had no ear there; upon which, she sagaciously perceived that he was the clipped housebreaker, who had married her with the intention of putting her to death. She immediately heated the poker and terminated his career, for which she was taken to King George upon his throne, and received the compliments of royalty on her great discretion and valour.

This same narrator, who had a Ghoulish pleasure, I have long been persuaded, in terrifying me to the utmost confines of my reason, had another authentic anecdote within her own experience, founded, I now believe, upon Raymond and Agnes or the Bleeding Nun.[13] She said it happened to her brother-in-law, who was immensely rich – which my father was not; and immensely tall – which my father was not. It was always a point with this Ghoule to present my dearest relations and friends to my youthful mind, under circumstances of disparaging contrast. The brother-in-law was riding once, through a forest, on a magnificent horse (we had no magnificent horse at our house), attended by a favourite and valuable Newfoundland dog (we had no dog), when he found himself benighted, and came to an Inn. A dark woman opened the door, and he asked her if he could have a bed there? She answered yes, and put his horse in the stable, and took him into a room where there were two dark men. While he was at supper, a parrot in the room began to talk, saying, 'Blood, blood! Wipe up the blood!' Upon which, one of the dark men wrung the parrot's neck, and said he was fond of roasted parrots, and he meant to have this one for breakfast in the morning. After eating and drinking heartily, the immensely rich tall brother-in-law went up to bed; but, he was rather vexed, because they had shut his dog in the stable, saying that they never allowed dogs in the house. He sat very quiet for more than an hour, thinking and thinking, when, just as his candle was burning out, he heard a scratch at the door. He opened the door, and there was the Newfoundland dog! The dog came softly in, smelt about him, went straight to some straw in a corner which the dark men had said covered apples, tore the straw away, and disclosed two sheets steeped in blood. Just at that moment the candle went out, and the brother-in-law, looking through a chink in the door, saw the two dark men stealing upstairs; one armed with a dagger, that long (about five feet); the other carrying a chopper, a sack, and a spade. Having no remembrance of the close of this adventure, I suppose my faculties to have been always so frozen with terror at this stage of it, that the power of listening stagnated within me for some quarter of an hour.

These barbarous stories carried me, sitting there on the Holly-Tree hearth, to the Roadside Inn, renowned in my time in a sixpenny book with a folding plate, representing in a central compartment of oval form the portrait of Jonathan Bradford, and in four corner compartments four incidents of the tragedy with which the name is associated – coloured with a hand at once so free and economical, that the bloom of Jonathan's complexion passed without any pause into the breeches of the ostler, and, smearing itself off into the next division, became rum in a bottle. Then, I remembered how the landlord was found at the murdered traveller's bedside, with his own knife at his feet, and blood upon his hand; how he was hanged for the murder, notwithstanding his protestation, that he had indeed come there to kill the traveller for his saddlebags, but had been stricken motionless on finding him already slain; and how the ostler, years afterwards, owned the deed.[14] By this time I had made myself quite uncomfortable. I stirred the fire, and stood with my back to it, as long as I could bear the heat, looking up at the darkness beyond the screen, and at the wormy curtains creeping in and creeping out, like the worms in the ballad of Alonzo the Brave and the fair Imogene.[15]

There was an Inn in the cathedral town where I went to school, which had pleasanter recollections about it than any of these. I took it next. It was the Inn where friends used to put up, and where we used to go to see parents, and to have salmon and fowls, and be tipped. It had an ecclesiastical sign – the Mitre[16] – and a bar that seemed to be the next best thing to a bishopric, it was so snug. I loved the landlord's youngest daughter to distraction – but let that pass. It was in this Inn that I was cried over by my rosy little sister, because I had acquired a black eye in a fight. And though she had been, that Holly-Tree night, for many a long year where all tears are dried, the Mitre softened me yet.

'To be continued, tomorrow,' said I, when I took my candle to go to bed. But, my bed took it upon itself to continue the train of thought that night. It carried me away, like the enchanted carpet,[17] to a distant place (though still in England), and there, alighting from a stagecoach at another Inn in the snow, as I had actually done some years before, I repeated in my sleep, a curious experience I had really had there. More than a year before I made the journey in the course of which I put up at that Inn, I had lost a very near and dear friend by death. Every night since, at home or away from home, I had dreamed of that friend; sometimes, as still living; sometimes, as returning from the world of shadows to comfort me; always, as being beautiful, placid, and happy; never in association with any approach to fear or distress. It was at a lonely Inn in a wide moorland place, that I halted to pass the night. When I had looked from my bedroom window over the waste of snow on which the moon was shining, I sat down by my fire to write a letter. I had always, until that hour, kept it within my own breast that I dreamed every night of the dear lost one. But, in the letter that I wrote, I recorded the circumstance, and added that I felt much interested in proving whether the subject of my dream would still be faithful to me, travel-tired, and in that remote place. No. I lost the beloved figure of my vision in parting with the secret. My sleep has never looked upon it since, in sixteen years, but once. I was in Italy, and awoke (or seemed to awake), the well-remembered voice distinctly in my ears, conversing with it. I entreated it, as it rose above my bed and soared up to the vaulted roof of the old room, to answer me a question I had asked, touching the Future Life. My hands were still outstretched towards it as it vanished, when I heard a bell ringing by the garden wall, and a voice, in the deep stillness of the night, calling on all good Christians to pray for the souls of the dead; it being All Souls Eve.

To return to the Holly-Tree. When I awoke next day, it was freezing hard, and the lowering sky threatened more snow. My breakfast cleared away, I drew my chair into its former place, and, with the fire getting so much the better of the landscape that I sat in twilight, resumed my Inn remembrances.

That was a good Inn down in Wiltshire where I put up once, in the days of the hard Wiltshire ale, and before all beer was bitterness.[18] It was on the skirts of Salisbury Plain, and the midnight wind that rattled my lattice window, came moaning at me from Stonehenge. There was a hanger-on at that establishment (a supernaturally preserved Druid, I believe him to have been, and to be still), with long white hair, and a flinty blue eye always looking afar off: who claimed to have been a shepherd, and who seemed to be ever watching for the reappearance on the verge of the horizon, of some ghostly flock of sheep that had been mutton for many ages. He was a man with a weird belief in him that no one could count the stones of Stonehenge twice, and make the same number of them;[19] likewise, that any one who counted them three times nine times, and then stood in the centre and said 'I dare!' would behold a tremendous apparition, and be stricken dead. He pretended to have seen a bustard (I suspect him to have been familiar with the dodo[20]), in manner following: He was out upon the plain at the close of a late autumn day, when he dimly discerned, going on before him at a curious fitfully bounding pace, what he at first supposed to be a gig-umbrella that had been blown from some conveyance, but what he presently believed to be a lean dwarf man upon a little pony. Having followed this object for some distance without gaining on it, and having called to it many times without receiving any answer, he pursued it for miles and miles, when, at length coming up with it, he discovered it to be the last bustard in Great Britain, degenerated into a wingless state, and running along the ground. Resolved to capture him or perish in the attempt, he closed with the bustard; but, the bustard, who had formed a counter resolution that he should do neither, threw him, stunned him, and was last seen making off due west. This weird man at that stage of metempsychosis, may have been a sleepwalker, or an enthusiast, or a robber; but, I awoke one night to find him in the dark at my bedside, repeating the Athanasian Creed[21] in a terrific voice. I paid my bill next day, and retired from the county with all possible precipitation.

That was not a commonplace story which worked itself out at a little Inn in Switzerland, while I was staying there. It was a very homely place, in a village of one narrow, zig-zag street among mountains, and you went in at the main door through the cow-house, and among the mules and the dogs and the fowls, before ascending a great bare staircase to the rooms: which were all of unpainted wood, without plastering or papering – like rough packing-cases. Outside, there was nothing but the straggling street, a little toy church with a copper-coloured steeple, a pine forest, a torrent, mists, and mountainsides. A young man belonging to this Inn, had dis-appeared eight weeks before (it was wintertime), and was supposed to have had some undiscovered love affair, and to have gone for a soldier. He had got up in the night, and dropped into the village street from the loft in which he slept with another man; and he had done it so quietly, that his companion and fellow labourer had heard no movement when he was awakened in the morning, and they said 'Louis, where is Henri?' They looked for him high and low, in vain, and gave him up. Now, outside this Inn there stood, as there stood outside every dwelling in the village, a stack of firewood; but, the stack belonging to the Inn was higher than any of the rest, because the Inn was the richest house and burnt the most fuel. It began to be noticed, while they were looking high and low, that a Bantam cock, part of the livestock of the Inn, put himself wonderfully out of his way to get to the top of this woodstack; and that he would stay there for hours and hours, crowing, until he appeared in danger of splitting himself. Five weeks went on – six weeks – and still this terrible Bantam, neglecting his domestic affairs, was always on the top of the woodstack, crowing the very eyes out of his head. By this time it was perceived that Louis had become inspired with a violent animosity towards the terrible Bantam, and one morning he was seen by a woman who sat nursing her goître at a little window in a gleam of sun, to catch up a rough billet of wood, with a great oath, hurl it at the terrible Bantam crowing on the woodstack, and bring him down dead. Hereupon, the woman, with a sudden light in her mind, stole round to the back of the woodstack, and, being a good climber, as all those women are, climbed up, and soon was seen upon the summit, screaming, looking down the hollow within, and crying, 'Seize Louis, the murderer! Ring the church bell! Here is the body!' I saw the murderer that day, and I saw him as I sat by my fire at the Holly-Tree Inn, and I see him now, lying shackled with cords on the stable litter, among the mild eyes and the smoking breath of the cows, waiting to be taken away by the police, and stared at by the fearful village. A heavy animal – the dullest animal in the stables – with a stupid head, and a lumpish face devoid of any trace of sensibility, who had been, within the knowledge of the murdered youth, an embezzler of certain small moneys belonging to his master, and who had taken this hopeful mode of putting a possible accuser out of his way. All of which he confessed next day, like a sulky wretch who couldn't be troubled any more, now that they had got hold of him and meant to make an end of him. I saw him once again, on the day of my departure from the Inn. In that Canton the headsman still does his office with a sword; and I came upon this murderer sitting bound to a chair, with his eyes bandaged, on a scaffold in a little marketplace. In that instant a great sword (loaded with quicksilver in the thick part of the blade), swept round him like a gust of wind, or fire, and there was no such creature in the world. My wonder was – not that he was so suddenly dispatched, but that any head was left unreaped, within a radius of fifty yards of that tremendous sickle.

That was a good Inn, too, with the kind, cheerful landlady and the honest landlord, where I lived in the shadow of Mont Blanc, and where one of the apartments has a zoological papering on the walls, not so accurately joined, but that the elephant occasionally rejoices in a tiger's hind legs and tail; while the lion puts on a trunk and tusks; and the bear, moulting[22] as it were, appears as to portions of himself like a leopard. I made several American friends at that Inn, who all called Mont Blanc, Mount Blank – except one good-humored gentleman, of a very sociable nature, who became on such intimate terms with it that he spoke of it familiarly as 'Blank;' observing at breakfast, 'Blank looks pretty tall this morning;'

or considerably doubting in the courtyard in the evening, whether there warn't some go-ahead naters in our country, sir, that would make out the top of Blank in a couple of hours from first start – now!

Once, I passed a fortnight at an Inn in the North of England, where I was haunted by the ghost of a tremendous pie. It was a Yorkshire pie, like a fort – an abandoned fort with nothing in it; but the waiter had a fixed idea that it was a point of ceremony at every meal, to put the pie on the table. After some days, I tried to hint, in several delicate ways, that I considered the pie done with; as, for example, by emptying fag-ends of glasses of wine into it; putting cheese-plates and spoons into it, as into a basket; putting wine bottles into it, as into a cooler; but always in vain, the pie being invariably cleaned out again and brought up as before. At last, beginning to be doubtful whether I was not the victim of a spectral illusion, and whether my health and spirits might not sink under the horrors of an imaginary pie, I cut a triangle out of it, fully as large as the musical instrument of that name in a powerful orchestra. Human prevision could not have foreseen the result – but the waiter mended the pie. With some effectual species of cement, he adroitly fitted the triangle in again, and I paid my reckoning and fled.

The Holly-Tree was getting rather dismal. I made an overland expedition beyond the screen, and penetrated as far as the fourth window. Here, I was driven back by stress of weather. Arrived at my winter quarters once more, I made up the fire, and took another Inn.

It was in the remotest part of Cornwall. A great annual Miners' Feast was being holden at the Inn, when I and my travelling companions presented ourselves at night among the wild crowd that were dancing before it by torchlight. We had

had a breakdown in the dark, on a stony morass some miles away; and I had the honor of leading one of the unharnessed post-horses. If any lady or gentleman, on perusal of the present lines, will take any very tall post-horse with his traces hanging about his legs, and will conduct him by the bearing-rein into the heart of a country dance of a hundred and fifty couples, that lady or gentleman will then, and only then, form an adequate idea of the extent to which that post-horse will tread on his conductor's toes. Over and above which, the post-horse, finding three hundred people whirling about him, will probably rear, and also lash out with his hind legs, in a manner incompatible with dignity or self-respect on his conductor's part. With such little drawbacks on my usually impressive aspect, I appeared at this Cornish Inn, to the unutterable wonder of the Cornish Miners. It was full, and twenty times full, and nobody could be received but the post-horse – though to get rid of that noble animal was something. While my fellow travellers and I were discussing how to pass the night and so much of the next day as must intervene before the jovial blacksmith and the jovial wheelwright would be in a condition to go out on the morass and mend the coach, an honest man stepped forth from the crowd and proposed his unlet floor of two rooms, with supper of eggs and bacon, ale and punch. We joyfully accompanied him home to the strangest of clean houses, where we were well entertained to the satisfaction of all parties. But, the novel feature of the entertainment was, that our host was a chairmaker, and that the chairs assigned to us were mere frames, altogether without bottoms of any sort; so that we passed the evening on perches. Nor was this the absurdest consequence; for when we unbent at supper, and any one of us gave way to laughter, he forgot the peculiarity of his position, and instantly disappeared. I myself, doubled up into an attitude from which self-extrication was impossible, was taken out of my frame, like a Clown in a comic pantomime who has tumbled into a tub, five times by the taper's light during the eggs and bacon.

The Holly-Tree was fast reviving within me a sense of loneliness. I began to feel conscious that my subject would never carry me on until I was dug out. I might be a week here – weeks!

There was a story with a singular idea in it, connected with an Inn I once passed a night at, in a picturesque old town on the Welch border. In a large, double-bedded room of this Inn, there had been a suicide committed by poison, in one bed, while a tired traveller slept unconscious in the other. After that time, the suicide bed was never used, but the other constantly was; the disused bedstead remaining in the room empty, though as to all other respects in its old state. The story ran, that whosoever slept in this room, though never so entire a stranger, from never so far off, was invariably observed to come down in the morning with an impression that he smelt Laudanum;[23] and that his mind always turned upon the subject of suicide; to which, whatever kind of man he might be, he was certain to make some reference if he conversed with any one. This went on for years, until it at length induced the landlord to take the disused bedstead down, and bodily burn it – bed, hangings, and all. The strange influence (this was the story), now changed to a fainter one, but never changed afterwards. The occupant of that room, with occasional but very rare exceptions, would come down in the morning, trying to recall a forgotten dream he had had in the night. The landlord, on his mentioning his perplexity, would suggest various commonplace subjects, not one of which, as he very well knew, was the true subject. But the moment the landlord suggested 'Poison,' the traveller started, and cried 'Yes!' He never failed to accept that suggestion, and he never recalled any more of the dream.

This reminiscence brought the Welch Inns in general, before me; with the women in their round hats, and the harpers with their white bears (venerable, but humbugs, I am afraid), playing outside the door while I took my dinner.[24] The transition was natural to the Highland Inns, with the oatmeal bannocks, the honey, the venison steaks, the trout from the loch, the whiskey, and perhaps (having the materials so temptingly at hand) the Athol brose.[25] Once, was I coming south from the Scottish Highlands in hot haste, hoping to change quickly at the station at the bottom of a certain wild historical glen, when these eyes did with mortification see the landlord come out with a telescope and sweep the whole prospect for the horses: which horses were away picking up their own living, and did not heave in sight under four hours. Having thought of the loch-trout I was taken by quick association to the Anglers' Inns of England (I have assisted at innumerable feats of angling, by lying in the bottom of the boat, whole summer days, doing nothing with the greatest perseverance: which I have generally found to be as effectual toward the taking of fish as the finest tackle and the utmost science); and to the pleasant white, clean, flower-pot-decorated bedrooms of those inns, overlooking the river, and the ferry, and the green ait,[26] and the church spire, and the country bridge; and to the peerless Emma with the bright eyes and the pretty smile who waited, bless her! with a natural grace that would have converted Blue Beard.[27] Casting my eyes upon my Holly-Tree fire, I next discerned among the glowing coals, the pictures of a score or more of those wonderful English posting-inns which we are all so sorry to have lost, which were so large and so comfortable, and which were such monuments of the British submission to rapacity and extortion. He who would see these houses pining away, let him walk from Basingstoke or even Windsor to London, by way of Hounslow, and moralise on their perishing remains; the stables crumbling to dust; unsettled labourers and wanderers bivouacing in the outhouses; grass growing in the yards; the rooms where erst so many hundred beds of down were made up, let off to Irish lodgers at eighteen pence a week; a little ill-looking beer shop shrinking in the tap of former days, burning coach-house gates for firewood, having one of its two windows bunged up, as if it had received punishment in a fight with the Railroad; a low, bandy-legged, brick-making bulldog standing in the doorway. What could I next see in my fire, so naturally, as the new railway-house of these times near the dismal country station; with nothing particular on draught but cold air and damp, nothing worth mentioning in the larder but new mortar, and no business doing, beyond a conceited affectation of luggage in the hall?

Then, I came to the Inns of Paris, with the pretty appartement of four pieces up one hundred and seventy-five waxed stairs, the privilege of ringing the bell all day long without influencing anybody's mind or body but your own, and the not-too-much-for-dinner, considering the price. Next, to the provincial Inns of France, with the great church tower rising above the courtyard, the horse bells jingling merrily up and down the street beyond, and the clocks of all descriptions in all the rooms, which are never right, unless taken at the precise minute when by getting exactly twelve hours too fast or too slow, they unintentionally become so. Away I went, next, to the lesser roadside Inns of Italy; where all the dirty clothes in the house (not in wear) are always lying in your ante-room; where the mosquitoes make a raisin pudding of your face in summer, and the cold bites it blue in winter; where you get what you can, and forget what you can't; where I should again like to be boiling my tea in a pocket-handkerchief dumpling, for want of a teapot. So, to the old palace Inns and old monastery Inns, in towns and cities of the same bright country; with their massive quadrangular stair-cases whence you may look from among clustering pillars high into the blue vault of Heaven; with their stately banqueting rooms, and vast refectories; with their labyrinths of ghostly bedchambers, and their glimpses into gorgeous streets that have no appearance of reality or possibility. So, to the close little Inns of the Malaria districts, with their pale attendants, and their peculiar smell of never letting in the air. So, to the immense fantastic Inns of Venice, with the cry of the gondolier below, as he skims the corner; the grip of the watery odors on one particular little bit of the bridge of your nose (which is never released while you stay there); and the great bell of St Mark's Cathedral tolling midnight. Next, I put up for a minute at the restless Inns upon the Rhine, where your going to bed, no matter at what hour, appears to be the tocsin for everybody else's getting up; and where, in the table d'hôte room at the end of the long table (with several Towers of Babel on it at the other end, all made of white plates),[28] one knot of stoutish men, entirely drest in jewels and dirt, and having nothing else upon them, *will* remain all night, clinking glasses, and singing about the river that flows and the grape that grows and Rhine wine that beguiles and Rhine woman that smiles and hi drink drink my friend and ho drink drink my brother, and all the rest of it. I departed thence, as a matter of course, to other German Inns, where all the eatables are sodden down to the same flavor, and where the mind is disturbed by the apparition of hot puddings, and boiled cherries sweet and slab, at awfully unexpected periods of the repast. After a draught of sparkling beer from a foaming glass jug, and a glance of recognition through the windows of the student beer-houses at Heidelberg and elsewhere, I put out to sea for the Inns of America, with their four hundred beds apiece, and their eight or nine hundred ladies and gentlemen at dinner every day. Again, I stood in the bar rooms thereof, taking my evening cobbler, julep, sling, or cocktail.[29] Again, I listened to my friend the General – whom I had known for five minutes, in the course of which period he had made me intimate for life with two Majors, who again had made me intimate for life with three Colonels, who again had made me brother to twenty-two civilians – again, I say, I listened to my friend the General, leisurely expounding the resources of the establishment, as to gentlemen's morning room, sir; ladies' morning room, sir; gentlemen's evening room, sir; ladies' evening room, sir; ladies' and gentlemen's evening room, sir; music room, sir; reading room, sir; over four-hundred sleeping rooms, sir; and the entire planned and finited within twelve calendar months from the first clearing off of the old incumbrances on the plot at a cost of five hundred thousand dollars, sir. Again I found, as to my individual way of thinking, that the greater, the more gorgeous, and the more dollarous, the establishment was, the less desirable it was. Nevertheless, again I drank my cobbler, julep, sling, or cocktail, in all goodwill to my friend the General, and my friends the Majors, Colonels, and civilians, all; full-well knowing that whatever little motes my beamy eyes may have descried in theirs, they belong to a kind, generous, large-hearted, and great people.[30]

I had been going on lately, at a quick pace, to keep my solitude out of my mind; but, here I broke down for good, and gave up the subject. What was I to do? What was to become of me? Into what extremity was I submissively to sink? Supposing that, like Baron Trenck,[31] I looked out for a mouse or spider, and found one, and beguiled my imprisonment by training it? Even that might be dangerous with a view to the future. I might be so far gone when the road did come to be cut through the snow, that, on my way forth, I might burst into tears, and beseech, like the prisoner who was released in his old age from the Bastille to be taken back again to the five windows, the ten curtains, and the sinuous drapery.[32]

A desperate idea came into my head. Under any other circumstances I should have rejected it; but in the strait at which I was, I held it fast. Could I so far overcome the inherent bashfulness which withheld me from the landlord's table and the company I might find there, as to make acquaintance, under various pretences, with some of the inmates of the house, singly – with the object of getting from each, either a whole autobiography or, a passage or experience in one, with which I could cheat the tardy time; first of all by seeking out, then by listening to, then by remembering and writing down? Could I, I asked myself, so far overcome my retiring nature as to do this? I could. I would. I did.[33]

The results of this conception I proceed to give, in the exact order in which I attained them. I began my plan of operations at once, and, by slow approaches and after overcoming many obstacles (all of my own making, I believe), reached the story of:

THE OSTLER
[by Wilkie Collins]

I find an old man, fast asleep, in one of the stalls of the stable. It is mid-day, and rather a strange time for an ostler to devote to sleep. Something curious, too, about the man's face. A withered, woe-begone face. The eyebrows painfully contracted; the mouth fast set, and drawn down at the corners; the hollow cheeks sadly, and, as I cannot help fancying, prematurely wrinkled; the scanty, grizzled hair, telling weakly its own tale of some past sorrow or suffering. How fast he draws his breath, too, for a man asleep! He is talking in his sleep.

'Wake up!' I hear him say, in a quick whisper through his fast clenched teeth. 'Wake up there! Murder! O Lord help me! Lord help me, alone in this place!'

He stops, and sighs again – moves one lean arm slowly, till it rests over his throat – shudders a little, and turns on his straw – the arm leaves his throat – the hand stretches itself out, and clutches at the side towards which he has turned, as if he fancies himself to be grasping at the edge of something. Is he waking? No – there is the whisper again; he is still talking in his sleep.

'Light grey eyes,' he says now, 'and a droop in the left eyelid. Yes! yes! – flaxen hair with a gold-yellow streak in it – all right, mother – fair, white arms with a down on them – little lady's hand, with a reddish look under the fingernails – and the knife – always the cursed knife – first on one side, then on the other. Aha! you she-devil, where's the knife? Never mind, mother – too late now. I've promised to marry, and marry I must. Murder! wake up there! for God's sake, wake up!'

At the last words his voice rises, and he grows so restless on a sudden, that I draw back quietly to the door. I see him shudder on the straw – his withered face grows distorted – he throws up both his hands with a quick, hysterical gasp; they strike against the bottom of the manger under which he lies; the blow awakens him; I have just time to slip through the door, before his eyes are fairly open and his senses are his own again.

What I have seen and heard has so startled and shocked me, that I feel my heart beating fast, as I softly and quickly retrace my steps across the inn-yard. The discomposure that is going on within me, apparently shows itself in my face; for, as I get back to the covered way leading to the Inn stairs, the landlord, who is just coming out of the house to ring some bell in the yard, stops astonished, and asks what is the matter with me? I tell him what I have just seen.

'Aha?' says the landlord, with an air of relief. 'I understand now. Poor old chap! He was only dreaming his old dream over again. There's the queerest story – of a dreadful kind, too, mind you – connected with him and his dream, that ever was told.'

I entreat the landlord to tell me the story. After a little hesitation, he complies with my request.

Some years ago, there lived in the suburbs of a large seaport town, on the west coast of England, a man in humble circumstances, by name Isaac Scatchard. His means of subsistence were derived from any employment that he could get, as an ostler; and, occasionally, when times went well with him, from temporary engagements in service, as stable-helper in private houses. Though a faithful, steady, and honest man, he got on badly in his calling. His ill-luck was proverbial among his neighbours. He was always missing good opportunities, by no fault of his own; and always living longest in service with amiable people who were not punctual payers of wages. 'Unlucky Isaac' was his nickname in his own neighbourhood – and no one could say that he did not richly deserve it.

With far more than one man's fair share of adversity to endure, Isaac had but one consolation to support him – and that was of the dreariest and most negative kind. He had no wife and children to increase his anxieties and add to the bitterness of his various failures in life. It might have been from mere insensibility, or it might have been from generous unwillingness to involve another in his own unlucky destiny – but the fact undoubtedly was, that he arrived at the middle term of life without marrying; and, what is much more remarkable, without once exposing himself, from eighteen to eight and thirty, to the genial imputation of ever having had a sweatheart. When he was out of service, he lived alone with his widowed mother. Mrs Scatchard was a woman above the average in her lowly station, as to capacities and manners. She had seen better days, as the phrase is; but she never referred to them in the presence of curious visitors; and though perfectly polite to every one who approached her, never cultivated any intimacies among her neighbours. She contrived to provide hardly enough, for her simple wants, by doing rough work for the tailors; and always managed to keep a decent home for her son to return to, whenever his ill luck drove him out helpless into the world.

One bleak autumn, when Isaac was getting on fast towards forty, and when he was, as usual, out of place, through no fault of his own, he set forth from his mother's cottage on a long walk inland to a gentleman's seat, where he had heard that a stable helper was required. It wanted then but two days of his birthday; and Mrs Scatchard, with her usual fondness, made him promise, before he started, that he would be back in time to keep that anniversary with her, in as festive a way as their poor means would allow. It was easy for him to comply with this request, even supposing he slept a night each way on the road. He was to start from home on Monday morning; and whether he got the new place or not, he was to be back for his birthday dinner on Wednesday at two o'clock.

Arriving at his destination too late on the Monday night to make application for the stable helper's place, he slept at the village inn, and, in good time on the Tuesday morning, presented himself at the gentleman's house, to fill the vacant situation. Here, again, his ill luck pursued him as inexorably as ever. The excellent written testimonials, as to character, which he was able to produce, availed him nothing; his long walk had been taken in vain – only the day before, the stable helper's place had been given to another man.

Isaac accepted this new disappointment resignedly, and as a matter of course. Naturally slow in capacity, he had the bluntness of sensibility and phlegmatic patience of disposition which frequently distinguish men with sluggishly working mental powers. He thanked the gentleman's steward, with his usual quiet civility, for granting him an interview, and took his departure with no appearance of unusual depression in his face or manner. Before starting on his homeward walk, he made some enquiries at the inn, and ascertained that he might save a few miles, on his return, by following a new road. Furnished with full instructions, several times repeated, as to the various turnings he was to take, he set forth for his homeward journey, and walked on all day with one stoppage for bread and cheese. Just as it was getting towards dark, the rain came on and the wind began to rise; and he found himself, to make matters worse, in a part of the country with which he was entirely unacquainted, though he knew himself to be some fifteen miles from home. The first house he found to enquire at was a lonely roadside inn, standing on the outskirts of a thick wood. Solitary as the place looked, it was welcome to a lost man who was also hungry, thirsty, footsore, and wet. The landlord was a civil, respectable-looking man; and the price he asked for a bed was reasonable enough. Isaac, therefore, decided on stopping comfortably at the inn for that night.

He was constitutionally a temperate man. His supper simply consisted of two rashers of bacon, a slice of homemade bread, and a pint of ale. He did not go to bed immediately after this moderate meal, but sat up with the landlord talking about his bad prospects and his long run of ill luck, and diverging from these topics to the subject of horseflesh and racing. Nothing was said either by himself, his host, or the few labourers who strayed into the taproom, which could, in the slightest degree, excite the very small and very dull imaginative family[34] which Isaac Scatchard possessed.

At a little after eleven the house was closed. Isaac went round with the landlord and held the candle while the doors and lower windows were being secured. He noticed with surprise the strength of the bolts, bars, and iron-sheathed shutters.

'You see we are rather lonely here,' said the landlord. 'We never have had any attempts made to break in yet, but it's always as well to be on the safe side. When nobody is sleeping here, I am the only man in the house. My wife and daughter are timid, and the servant girl takes after her missusses. Another glass of ale, before you turn in? – No! – Well, how such a sober man as you comes to be out of place is more than I can make out, for one. – Here's where you're to sleep. You're our only lodger tonight, and I think you'll say my missus has done her best to make you comfortable. You're quite sure you won't have another glass of ale? – Very well. Good night.'

It was half-past eleven by the clock in the passage as they went upstairs to the bedroom, the window of which looked on to the wood at the back of the house. Isaac locked the door, set his candle on the chest of drawers, and wearily got ready for bed. The bleak autumn wind was still blowing, and the solemn, monotonous, surging moan of it in the wood was dreary and awful to hear through the night silence. Isaac felt strangely wakeful, and resolved, as he lay down in bed, to keep the candle alight until he began to grow sleepy; for there was something unendurably depressing in the bare idea of lying awake in the darkness, listening to the dismal, ceaseless moaning of the wind in the wood.

Sleep stole on him before he was aware of it. His eyes closed, and he fell off insensibly to rest, without having so much as thought of extinguishing the candle.

The first sensation of which he was conscious after sinking into slumber, was a strange shivering that ran through him suddenly from head to foot, and a dreadful sinking pain at the heart, such as he had never felt before. The shivering only disturbed his slumbers – the pain woke him instantly. In one moment he passed from a state of sleep to a state of wakefulness – his eyes wide open – his mental perceptions cleared on a sudden as if by a miracle.

The candle had burnt down nearly to the last morsel of tallow; but the top of the unsnuffed wick had just fallen off, and the light in the little room was, for the moment, fair and full. Between the foot of his bed and the closed door there stood a woman with a knife in her hand, looking at him. He was stricken speechless with terror, but he did not lose the preternatural clearness of his faculties; and he never took his eyes off the woman. She said not one word as they stared each other in the face; but she began to move slowly towards the left-hand side of the bed.

His eyes followed her. She was a fair, fine woman, with yellowish flaxen hair, and light grey eyes, with a droop in the left eyelid. He noticed those things and fixed them on his mind, before she was round at the side of the bed. Speechless, with no expression in her face, with no noise following her footfall, – she came closer and closer – stopped and slowly raised the knife. He raised his right arm over his throat to save it; but as he saw the knife coming down, threw his hand across the bed to the right side, and jerked his body over that way, just as the knife descended on the mattress within an inch of his shoulder.

His eyes fixed on her arm and hand, as she slowly drew the knife out of the bed. A white, well-shaped arm, with a pretty down lying lightly over the fair skin. A delicate lady's hand, with the crowning beauty of a pink flush under and round the fingernails.

She drew the knife out, and passed back again slowly to the foot of the bed; stopped there for a moment looking at him; then came on – still speechless, still with no expression on the blank, beautiful face, still with no sound following the stealthy footfalls – came on to the right side of the bed where he now lay. As she approached, she raised the knife again, and he drew himself away to the left side. She struck, as before, right into the mattress, with a deliberate, perpendicularly-downward action of the arm. This time his eyes wandered from her to the knife. It was like the large clasp knives which he had often seen labouring men use to cut their bread and bacon with. Her delicate little fingers did not conceal more than two thirds of the handle; he noticed that it was made of buck-horn, clean and shining as the blade was, and looking like new.

For the second time she drew the knife out, concealed it in the wide sleeve of her gown, then stopped by the bedside, watching him. For an instant he saw her standing in that position – then the wick of the spent candle fell over into the socket. The flame diminished to a little blue point, and the room grew dark. A moment, or less, if possible, passed so – and then the wick flamed up, smokily for the last time. His eyes were still looking eagerly over the right-hand side of the bed when the final flash of light came, but they discerned nothing. The fair woman with the knife was gone.

The conviction that he was alone again, weakened the hold of the terror that had struck him dumb up to this time. The preternatural sharpness which the very intensity of his panic had mysteriously imparted to his faculties, left them suddenly. His brain grew confused – his heart beat wildly – his ears opened for the first time since the appearance of the woman, to a sense of the woful, ceaseless moaning of the wind among the trees. With the dreadful conviction of the reality of what he had seen, still strong within him, he leaped out of bed, and screaming –'Murder: – Wake up, there, wake up!' – dashed headlong through the darkness to the door.

It was fast locked, exactly as he had left it on going to bed.

His cries on starting up, had alarmed the house. He heard the terrified, confused exclamations of women; he saw the master of the house approaching along the passage, with his burning rush-candle[35] in one hand and his gun in the other.

'What is it?' asked the landlord, breathlessly.

Isaac could only answer in a whisper: 'A woman, with a knife in her hand,' he gasped out. 'In my room, a fair, yellow-haired woman; she jobbed at me with the knife, twice over.'

The landlord's pale cheeks grew paler. He looked at Isaac eagerly by the flickering light of his candle; his face began to get red again – his voice altered, too, as well as his complexion.

'She seems to have missed you twice,' he said.

'I dodged the knife as it came down,' Isaac went on, in the same scared whisper. 'It struck the bed each time.'

The landlord took his candle into the bedroom immediately. In less than a minute he came out again into the passage in a violent passion.

'The devil fly away with you and your woman with the knife! What do you mean by coming into a man's place and frightening his family out of their wits about a dream?'

'I'll leave your house,' said Isaac, faintly. 'Better out on the road, in rain and dark, on my way home, than back again in that room after what I've seen in it. Lend me a light to get on my clothes by, and tell me what I'm to pay.'

'Pay!' cried the landlord, leading the way with his light sulkily into the bedroom. 'You'll find your score on the slate when you go downstairs. I wouldn't have taken you in for all the money you've got about you, if I'd known your dreaming, screeching ways beforehand. Look at the bed. Where's the cut of a knife in it? Look at the window – is the lock bursted? Look at the door (which I heard you fasten myself) – is it broke in? A murdering woman with a knife in my house! You ought to be ashamed of yourself!'

Isaac answered not a word. He huddled on his clothes; and then they went downstairs together.

'Nigh on twenty minutes past two!' said the landlord, as they passed the clock. 'A nice time in the morning to frighten honest people out of their wits!'

Isaac paid his bill, and the landlord let him out at the front door, asking, with a grin of contempt, as he undid the strong fastenings, whether 'the murdering woman got in that way?'

They parted without a word on either side. The rain had ceased; but the night was dark, and the wind bleaker than ever. Little did the darkness, or the cold, or the uncertainty about his way home, matter to Isaac. If he had been turned out into a wilderness in a thunderstorm, it would have been a relief, after what he had suffered in the bedroom of the inn.

What was the fair woman with the knife? The creature of a dream, or that other creature from the unknown world called among men by the name of ghost? He could make nothing of the mystery – had made nothing of it, even when it was mid-day on Wednesday, and when he stood, at last, after many times missing his road, once more on the doorstep of home.

His mother came out eagerly to receive him. His face told her in a moment that something was wrong.

'I've lost the place; but that's my luck. I dreamed an ill dream last night, mother – or, may be I saw a ghost. Take it either way, it scared me out of my senses, and I'm not my own man again yet.'

'Isaac! your face frightens me. Come in to the fire. Come in, and tell mother all about it.'

He was as anxious to tell as she was to hear; for it had been his hope, all the way home, that his mother, with her quicker capacity and superior knowledge, might be able to throw some light on the mystery which he could not clear up for himself. His memory of the dream was still mechanically vivid, though his thoughts were entirely confused by it.

His mother's face grew paler and paler as he went on. She never interrupted him by so much as a single word; but when he had done, she moved her chair close to his, put her arm round his neck, and said to him:

'Isaac, you dreamed your ill dream on this Wednesday morning. What time was it when you saw the fair woman with the knife in her hand?'

Isaac reflected on what the landlord had said when they passed by the clock on his leaving the inn – allowed as nearly as he could for the time that must have elapsed between the unlocking of his bedroom door and the paying of his bill just before going away, and answered:

'Somewhere about two o'clock in the morning.'

His mother suddenly quitted her hold of his neck, and struck her hands together with a gesture of despair.

'This Wednesday is your birthday Isaac; and two o'clock in the morning was the time when you were born!'

Isaac's capacities were not quick enough to catch the infection of his mother's superstitious dread. He was amazed and a little startled also, when she suddenly rose from her chair, opened her old writing desk, took out pen and ink and paper, and then said to him:

'Your memory is but a poor one, Isaac, and now I'm an old woman, mine's not much better. I want all about this dream of yours to be as well known to both of us, years hence, as it is now. Tell me over again all you told me a minute ago, when you spoke of what the woman with the knife looked like.'

Isaac obeyed, and marvelled much as he saw his mother carefully set down on paper the very words that he was saying. 'Light grey eyes,' she wrote, as they came to the descriptive part, 'with a droop in the left eyelid. Flaxen hair, with a gold-yellow streak in it. White arms, with a down on them. Little lady's hand, with a reddish look about the fingernails. Clasp knife with a buck-horn handle, that seemed as good as new.' To these particulars, Mrs Scatchard added the year, month, day of the week, and time in the morning, when the woman of the dream appeared to her son. She then locked up the paper carefully in her writing desk.

Neither on that day, nor on any day after, could her son induce her to return to the matter of the dream. She obstinately kept her thoughts about it to herself, and even refused to refer again to the paper in her writing desk. Ere long, Isaac grew weary of attempting to make her break her resolute silence; and time, which sooner or later, wears out all things, gradually wore out the impression produced on him by the dream. He began by thinking of it carelessly, and he ended by not thinking of it at all. This result was the more easily brought about by the advent of some important changes for the better in his prospects, which commenced not long after his terrible night's experience at the inn. He reaped at last the reward of his long and patient suffering under adversity, by getting an excellent place, keeping it for seven years, and leaving it, on the death of his master, not only with an excellent character, but also with a comfortable annuity bequeathed to him as a reward for saving his mistress's life in a carriage accident. Thus it happened that Isaac Scatchard returned to his old mother, seven years after the time of the dream at the inn, with an annual sum of money at his disposal, sufficient to keep them both in ease and independence for the rest of their lives.

The mother, whose health had been bad of late years, profited so much by the care bestowed on her, and by freedom from money anxieties, that when Isaac's next birthday came round, she was able to sit up comfortably at table and dine with him.

On that day, as the evening drew on, Mrs Scatchard discovered that a bottle of tonic medicine – which she was accustomed to take, and in which she had fancied that a dose or more was still left – happened to be empty, Isaac immediately volunteered to go to the chemist's, and get it filled again. It was as rainy and bleak an autumn night as on the memorable past occasion when he lost his way and slept at the roadside inn.

On going into the chemist's shop, he was passed hurriedly by a poorly dressed woman coming out of it. The glimpse he had of her face struck him, and he looked back after her as she descended the doorsteps.

'You're noticing that woman?' said the chemist's apprentice behind the counter. 'It's my opinion there's something wrong with her. She's been asking for laudanum to put to a bad tooth. Master's out for half an hour; and I told her I wasn't allowed to sell poison to strangers in his absence. She laughed in a queer way, and said she would come back in half an hour. If she expects master to serve her, I think she'll be disappointed. It's a case of suicide, sir, if ever there was one yet.'

These words added immeasurably to the sudden interest in the woman which Isaac had felt at the first sight of her face. After he had got the medicine bottle filled, he looked about anxiously for her, as soon as he was out in the street. She was walking slowly up and down on the opposite side of the road. With his heart, very much to his own surprise, beating fast, Isaac crossed over and spoke to her.

He asked if she was in any distress. She pointed to her torn shawl, her scanty dress, her crushed, dirty bonnet then moved under a lamp so as to let the light fall on her stern, pale, but still most beautiful face.

'I look like a comfortable, happy woman – don't I?' she said with a bitter laugh.

She spoke with a purity of intonation which Isaac had never heard before from other than ladies' lips. Her slightest actions seemed to have the easy negligent grace of a thoroughbred woman. Her skin, for all its poverty-stricken paleness, was as delicate as if her life had been passed in the enjoyment of every social comfort that wealth can purchase. Even her small, finely shaped hands, gloveless as they were, had not lost their whiteness.

Little by little, in answer to his question, the sad story of the woman came out. There is no need to relate it here; it is told over and over again in Police Reports and paragraphs about Attempted Suicides.

'My name is Rebecca Murdoch,' said the woman, as she ended. 'I have ninepence left, and I thought of spending it at the chemist's over the way in securing a passage to the other world. Whatever it is, it can't be worse to me than this – so why should I stop here?'

Besides the natural compassion and sadness moved in his heart by what he heard, Isaac felt within him some mysterious influence at work all the time the woman was speaking, which utterly confused his ideas, and almost deprived him of his powers of speech. All that he could say in answer to her last reckless words was, that he would prevent her from attempting her own life, if he followed her about all night to do it. His rough, trembling earnestness, seemed to impress her.

'I won't occasion you that trouble,' she answered, when he repeated his threat, 'You have given me a fancy for living by speaking kindly to me. No need for the mockery of protestations and promises. You may believe me without them. Come to Fuller's Meadow tomorrow at twelve and you will find me alive, to answer for myself. No! – no money. My ninepence will do to get me as good a night's lodging as I want.'

She nodded and left him. He made no attempt to follow – he felt no suspicion that she was deceiving him.

'It's strange, but I can't help believing her,' he said to himself – and walked away, bewildered, towards home.

On entering the house his mind was still so completely absorbed by its new subject of interest, that he took no notice of what his mother was doing when he came in with the bottle of medicine. She had opened her old writing desk in his absence, and was now reading a paper attentively that lay inside it. On every birthday of Isaac's since she had written down the particulars of his dream from his own lips, she had been accustomed to read that same paper, and ponder over it in private.

The next day he went to Fuller's Meadow. He had done only right in believing her so implicitly – she was there, punctual to a minute, to answer for herself. The last-left faint defences in Isaac's heart against the fascination which a word or look from her began inscrutably to exercise over him, sank down and vanished before her forever on that memorable morning.

When a man, previously insensible to the influence of women, forms an attachment in middle life, the instances are rare indeed, let the warning circumstances be what they may, in which he is found capable of freeing himself from the tyranny of the new ruling passion. The charm of being spoken to familiarly, fondly, and gratefully by a woman whose language and manners still retained enough of their early refinement to hint at the high social station that she had lost, would have been a dangerous luxury to a man of Isaac's rank at the age of twenty. But it was far more than that – it was certain ruin to him – now that his heart was opening unworthily to a new influence, at that middle time of life when strong feelings of all kinds, once implanted, strike root most stubbornly in a man's moral nature. A few more stolen interviews after that first morning in Fuller's Meadow completed his infatuation. In less than a month from the time when he first met her, Isaac Scatchard had consented to give Rebecca Murdoch a new interest in existence, and a chance of recovering the character she had lost, by promising to make her his wife.

She had taken possession, not of his passions only, but of his faculties as well. All arrangements for the present and all plans for the future were of her devising. All the mind he had he put into her keeping. She directed him on every point; even instructing him how to break the news of his approaching marriage in the safest manner to his mother.

'If you tell her how you met me and who I am at first,' said the cunning woman, 'she will move heaven and earth to prevent our marriage. Say I am the sister of one of your fellow servants – ask her to see me before you go into any more particulars – and leave it to me to do the rest. I want to make her love me next best to you, Isaac, before she knows anything of who I really am.'

The motive of the deceit was sufficient to sanctify it to Isaac. The stratagem proposed relieved him of his one great anxiety, and quieted his uneasy conscience on the subject of his mother. Still, there was something wanting to perfect his happiness, something that he could not realise, something mysteriously untraceable, and yet, something that perpetually made itself felt; not when he was absent from Rebecca Murdoch, but, strange to say, when he was actually in her presence! She was kindness itself with him; she never made him feel his inferior capacities, and inferior manners – she showed the sweetest anxiety to please him in the smallest trifles; but, in spite of all these attractions, he never could feel quite at his ease with her. At their first meeting, there had mingled with his admiration when he looked in her face, a faint involuntary feeling of doubt whether that face was entirely strange to him. No after familiarity had the slightest effect on this inexplicable wearisome uncertainty.

Concealing the truth as he had been directed, he announced his marriage engagement precipitately and confusedly to his mother on the day when he contracted it. Poor Mrs Scatchard showed her perfect confidence in her son by flinging her arms round his neck, and giving him joy of having found at last, in the sister of one of his fellow servants, a woman to comfort and care for him after his mother was gone. She was all eagerness to see the woman of her son's choice; and the next day was fixed for introduction.

It was a bright sunny morning, and the little cottage parlour was full of light as Mrs Scatchard, happy and expectant, dressed for the occasion in her Sunday gown, sat waiting for her son and her future daughter-in-law. Punctual to the appointed time, Isaac hurriedly and nervously led his promised wife into the room. His mother rose to receive her – advanced a few steps, smiling – looked Rebecca full in the eyes – and suddenly stopped. Her face, which had been flushed the moment before, turned white in an instant – her eyes lost their expression of softness and kindness, and assumed a blank look of terror – her outstretched hands fell to her sides, and she staggered back a few steps with a low cry to her son.

'Isaac!' she whispered, clutching him fast by the arm, when he asked alarmedly if she was taken ill. 'Isaac! Does that woman's face remind you of nothing?'

Before he could answer; before he could look around to where Rebecca, astonished and angered by her reception, stood, at the lower end of the room; his mother pointed impatiently to her writing desk, and gave him the key.

'Open it,' she said, in a quick, breathless whisper.

'What does this mean? Why am I treated as if I had no business here? Does your mother want to insult me?' asked Rebecca, angrily.

'Open it, and give me the paper in the left-hand drawer. Quick! quick, for Heaven's sake!' said Mrs Scatchard, shrinking further back in terror. Isaac gave her the paper. She looked over it eagerly for a moment – then followed Rebecca, who was now turning away haughtily to leave the room, and caught her by the shoulder – abruptly raised the long, loose sleeve of her gown, and glanced at her hand and arm. Something like fear began to steal over the angry expression of Rebecca's face as she shook herself free from the old woman's grasp. 'Mad!' she said to herself; 'and Isaac never told me.' With these few words she left the room.

Isaac was hastening after her when his mother turned and stopped his further progress. It wrung his heart to see the misery and terror in her face as she looked at him.

'Light grey eyes,' she said, in low, mournful, awe-struck tones, pointing towards the open door. 'A droop in the left eyelid. Flaxen hair with a gold-yellow streak in it. White arms with a down on them. Little, ladies' hand, with a reddish look under the fingernails. *The woman of the dream!* – Oh, Heaven! Isaac, the woman of the dream!'

That faint cleaving doubt which he had never been able to shake off in Rebecca Murdoch's presence, was fatally set at rest forever. He *had* seen her face, then, before – seven years before, on his birthday, in the bedroom of the lonely inn. 'The woman of the dream!'

'Be warned, Oh, my son! be warned! Isaac! Isaac! let her go, and do you stop with me!'

Something darkened the parlour window, as those words were said. A sudden chill ran through him; and he glanced sidelong at the shadow. Rebecca Murdoch had come back. She was peering in curiously at them over the low window blind.

'I have promised to marry, mother,' he said, 'and marry I must.'

The tears came into his eyes as he spoke, and dimmed his sight; but he could just discern the fatal face outside moving away again from the window.

His mother's head sank lower.

'Are you faint?' he whispered.

'Broken-hearted, Isaac.'

He stooped down and kissed her. The shadow, as he did so, returned to the window; and the fatal face peered in curiously once more.

Three weeks after that day, Isaac and Rebecca were man and wife. All that was hopelessly dogged and stubborn in the man's moral nature, seemed to have closed round his fatal passion, and to have fixed it unassailably in his heart.

After that first interview in the cottage parlour, no consideration would induce Mrs Scatchard to see her son's wife again, or even to talk of her when Isaac tried hard to plead her cause after their marriage. This course of conduct was not in any degree occasioned by a discovery of the degradation in which Rebecca had lived. There was no question of that between mother and son. There was no question of anything but the fearfully exact resemblance between the living breathing woman and the spectre woman of Isaac's dream. Rebecca, on her side, neither felt nor expressed the slightest sorrow at the estrangement between herself and her mother-in-law. Isaac, for the sake of peace, had never contradicted her first idea that age and long illness had affected Mrs Scatchard's mind. He even allowed his wife to upbraid him for not having confessed this to her at the time of their marriage engagement, rather than risk anything by hinting at the truth. The sacrifice of his integrity before his one all-mastering delusion, seemed but a small thing, and cost his conscience but little, after the sacrifices he had already made.

The time of waking from his delusion – the cruel and the rueful time – was not far off. After some quiet months of married life, as the summer was ending, and the year was getting on towards the month of his birthday, Isaac found his wife altering towards him. She grew sullen and contemptuous – she formed acquaintances of the most dangerous kind, in defiance of his objections, his entreaties, and his commands, – and, worst of all, she learnt ere long, after every fresh difference with her husband, to seek the deadly self-oblivion of drink. Little by little, after the first miserable discovery that his wife was keeping company with drunkards, the shocking certainty forced itself on Isaac that she had grown to be a drunkard herself.

He had been in a sadly desponding state for some time before the occurrence of these domestic calamities. His mother's health, as he could but too plainly discern every time he went to see her at the cottage, was failing fast; and he upbraided himself in secret as the cause of the bodily and mental suffering she endured. When, to his remorse on his mother's account, was added the shame and misery occasioned by the discovery of his wife's degradation, he sank under the double trial – his face began to alter fast, and he looked what he was, a spirit-broken man. His mother, still struggling bravely against the illness that was hurrying her to the grave, was the first to notice the sad alteration in him, and the first to hear of his last bitterest trouble with his wife. She could only weep bitterly, on the day when he made his humiliating confession; but on the next occasion when he went to see her, she had taken a resolution in reference to his domestic afflictions, which astonished, and even alarmed him. He found her dressed to go out, and on asking the reason, received this answer:

'I am not long for this world, Isaac,' said she; 'and I shall not feel easy on my deathbed, unless I have done my best to the last to make my son happy. I mean to put my own fears and my own feelings out of the question, and to go with you to your wife, and try what I can do to reclaim her. Give me your arm, Isaac; and let me do the last thing I can in this world to help my son before it is too late.'

He could not disobey her; and they walked together slowly towards his miserable home. It was only one o'clock in the afternoon when they reached the cottage where he lived. It was the dinner hour, and Rebecca was in the kitchen. He was thus able to take his mother quietly into the parlour, and then prepare his wife for the interview. She had fortunately drank but little at that early hour, and she was less sullen and capricious than usual. He returned to his mother with his mind tolerably at ease. His wife soon followed him into the parlour, and the meeting between her and Mrs Scatchard passed off better than he had ventured to anticipate: though he observed with secret apprehension, that his mother, resolutely as she controlled herself in other respects, could not look his wife in the face when she spoke to her. It was a relief to him, therefore, when Rebecca began to lay the cloth.

She laid the cloth – brought in the bread tray, and cut a slice from the loaf for her husband – then returned to the kitchen. At that moment, Isaac, still anxiously watching his mother, was startled by seeing the same ghastly change pass over her face, which had altered it so awfully on the morning when Rebecca and she first met. Before he could say a word she whispered with a look of horror: –

'Take me back! – home, home, again, Isaac! Come with me, and never come back again.'

He was afraid to ask for an explanation, – he could only sign to her to be silent, and help her quickly to the door. As they passed the bread tray on the table she stopped and pointed to it.

'Did you see what your wife cut your bread with?' she asked, in a low, still whisper.

'No mother, – I was not noticing – what was it?'

'Look!'

He did look. A new clasp knife, with a buck-horn handle lay with the loaf in the bread tray. He stretched out his hand, shudderingly, to possess himself of it; but, at the same time, there was a noise in the kitchen, and his mother caught at his arm.

'The knife of the dream! – Isaac, I'm faint with fear – take me away! before she comes back!'

He was hardly able to support her – the visible, tangible reality of the knife struck him with a panic, and utterly destroyed any faint doubts that he might have entertained up to this time, in relation to the mysterious dream-warning of nearly eight years before. By a last desperate effort, he summoned self-possession enough to help his mother quietly out of the house, – so quietly, that the 'dream-woman' (he thought of her by that name, now!) did not hear them departing, from the kitchen.

'Don't go back, Isaac – don't go back!' implored Mrs Scatchard, as he turned to go away, after seeing her safely seated again in her own room.

'I must get the knife,' he answered, under his breath. She tried to stop him again; but he hurried out without another word.

On his return, he found that his wife had discovered their secret departure from the house. She had been drinking, and was in a fury of passion. The dinner in the kitchen was flung under the grate; the cloth was off the parlour-table. Where was the knife? Unwisely, he asked for it. She was only too glad of the opportunity of irritating him, which the request afforded her. 'He wanted the knife, did he? Could he give her a reason why? – No! – Then he should not have it, – not if he went down on his knees to ask for it.' Further recriminations elicited the fact that she had bought it a bargain – and that she considered it her own especial property. Isaac saw the uselessness of attempting to get the knife by fair means, and determined to search for it, later in the day, in secret. The search was unsuccessful. Night came on, and he left the house to walk about the streets. He was afraid now to sleep in the same room with her.

Three weeks passed. Still sullenly enraged with him, she would not give up the knife; and still that fear of sleeping in the same room with her, possessed him. He walked about at night, or dozed in the parlour, or sat watching by his mother's bedside. Before the expiration of the first week in the new month his mother died. It wanted then but ten days of her son's birthday. She had longed to live till that anniversary. Isaac was present at her death; and her last words in this world were addressed to him: 'Don't go back, my son, don't go back!'

He was obliged to go back, if it were only to watch his wife. Exasperated to the last degree by his distrust of her, she had revengefully sought to add a sting to his grief, during the last days of his mother's illness, by declaring that she would assert her right to attend the funeral. In spite of all that he could do, or say, she held with wicked pertinacity to her word; and, on the day appointed for the burial, forced herself – inflamed and shameless with drink – into her husband's presence, and declared that she would walk in the funeral procession to his mother's grave.

This last worst outrage, accompanied by all that was most insulting in word and look, maddened him for the moment. He struck her. The instant the blow was dealt, he repented it. She crouched down, silent in a corner of the room, and eyed him steadily; it was a look that cooled his blood, and made him tremble. But there was no time now to think of a means of making atonement. Nothing remained, but to risk the worst till the funeral was over. There was but one way of making sure of her. He locked her into her bedroom.

When he came back some hours after, he found her sitting, very much altered in look and bearing, by the bedside, with a bundle on her lap. She rose, and faced him quietly, and spoke with a strange stillness in her voice, a strange repose in her eyes, a strange composure in her manner.

'No man has ever struck me twice,' she said, 'and my husband shall have no second opportunity. Set the door open and let me go. From this day forth we see each other no more.'

Before he could answer she passed him, and left the room. He saw her walk away up the street.

Would she return? All that night he watched and waited; but no footstep came near the house. The next night, over-powered by fatigue, he lay down in bed, in his clothes, with the door locked, the key on the table, and the candle burning. His slumber was not disturbed. The third night, the fourth, the fifth, the sixth, passed, and nothing happened. He lay down on the seventh; still in his clothes, still with the door locked, the key on the table, and the candle burning, but easier in his mind.

Easier in his mind, and in perfect health of body, when he fell off to sleep. But his rest was disturbed. He woke twice, without any sensation of uneasiness. But the third time it was that never-to-be-forgotten shivering of the night at the lonely inn, that dreadful sinking pain at the heart, which once more aroused him in an instant.

His eyes opened towards the left hand side of the bed, and there stood – The woman of the dream, again? – No! His wife; the living reality, with the dream-spectre's face – in the dream-spectre's attitude; the fair arm up – the knife clasped in the delicate, white hand.

He sprang upon her, almost at the instant of seeing her, and yet not quickly enough to prevent her from hiding the knife. Without a word from him – without a cry from her – he pinioned her in a chair. With one hand he felt up her sleeve – and, there, where the dream-woman had hidden the knife, she had hidden it, – the knife with the buck-horn handle, that looked like new.

In the despair of that fearful moment, his brain was steady, his heart was calm. He looked at her fixedly, with the knife in his hand, and said these last words:

'You told me we should see each other no more, and you have come back. It is my turn now, to go, and to go forever. *I* say that we shall see each other no more, and *my* word shall not be broken.'

He left her, and set forth into the night. There was a bleak wind abroad, and the smell of recent rain was in the air. The distant church clocks chimed the quarter as he walked rapidly beyond the last houses in the suburb. He asked the first policeman he met, what hour that was, of which the quarter past had just struck.

The man referred sleepily to his watch, and answered: 'Two o'clock.' Two in the morning. What day of the month was this day that had just begun? He reckoned it up from the date of his mother's funeral. The fatal parallel was complete – it was his birthday!

Had he escaped the mortal peril which his dream foretold? or had he only received a second warning? As that ominous doubt forced itself on his mind, he stopped, reflected, and turned back again towards the city. He was still resolute to hold to his word, and never to let her see him more; but there was a thought now in his mind of having her watched and followed. The knife was in his possession – the world was before him; but a new distrust of her – a vague, unspeakable, superstitious dread – had overcome him.

'I must know where she goes, now she thinks I have left her,' he said to himself, as he stole back wearily to the precincts of his house.

It was still dark. He had left the candle burning in the bedchamber; but when he looked up at the window of the room now, there was no light in it. He crept cautiously to the house door. On going away, he remembered to have closed it: on trying it now, he found it open.

He waited outside, never losing sight of the house, till daylight. Then he ventured indoors – listened, and heard nothing – looked into kitchen, scullery, parlour; and found nothing: went up, at last, into the bedroom – it was empty. A pick-lock lay on the floor, betraying how she had gained entrance in the night; and that was the only trace of her.

Whither had she gone? That no mortal tongue could tell him. The darkness had covered her flight; and when the day broke, no man could say where the light found her.

Before leaving the house and the town forever, he gave instructions to a friend and neighbour to sell his furniture for anything that it would fetch, and apply the proceeds to employing the police to trace her. The directions were honestly followed, and the money was all spent; but the enquiries led to nothing. The pick-lock on the bedroom floor remained the one last useless trace of her.

At this point of the narrative the landlord paused, and looked towards the stable door.

'So far,' he said, 'I tell you what was told to me. The little that remains to be added lies within my own experience. Between two and three months after the events I have just been relating, Isaac Scatchard came to me, withered and old-looking before his time, just as you saw him today. He had his testimonials to character with him, and he asked for employment here. I gave him a trial, and liked him in spite of his queer habits. He is as sober, honest, and willing a man as there is in England. As for his restlessness at night, and his sleeping away his leisure time in the day, who can wonder at it after hearing his story? Besides, he never objects to being roused up, when he's wanted, so there's not much inconvenience to complain of, after all.'

'I suppose he is afraid of waking out of that dreadful dream in the dark?' said I.

'No,' returned the landlord. 'The dream comes back to him so often, that he has got to bear with it by this time resignedly enough. It's his wife keeps him waking at night, as he has often told me.'

'What! Has she never been heard of yet?'

'Never. Isaac himself has the one perpetual thought about her, that she is alive, and looking for him. I believe he wouldn't let himself drop off to sleep towards two in the morning for a king's ransom. Two in the morning, he says, is the time when she will find him, one of these days. Two in the morning is the time, all the year round, when he likes to be most certain that he has got that clasp knife safe about him. He does not mind being alone, as long as he is awake, except on the night before his birthday, when he firmly believes himself to be in peril of his life. The birthday has only come round once since he has been here; and then he sat up, along with the night porter. 'She's looking for me,' he always says, when I speak to him on the one theme of his life; 'she's looking for me.' He may be right. She *may* be looking for him. Who can tell?'

'Who can tell!' said I.

THE BOOTS
[by Charles Dickens]

Where had he been in his time? he repeated when I asked him the question. Lord, he had been everywhere! And what had he been? Bless you, he had been everything you could mention a'most.

Seen a good deal? Why, of course he had. I should say so, he could assure me, if I only knew about a twentieth part of what had come in *his* way. Why, it would be easier for him, he expected, to tell what he hadn't seen, than what he had. Ah! A deal, it would.

What was the curiousest thing he had seen? Well! He didn't know. He couldn't momently name what was the curiousest thing he had seen – unless it was a Unicorn – and he see *him* once, at a Fair. But, supposing a young gentleman not eight year old, was to run away with a fine young woman of seven, might I think *that* a queer start? Certainly? Then, that was a start as he himself had had his blessed eyes on – and he had cleaned the shoes they run away in – and they was so little that he couldn't get his hand into 'em.

Master Harry Walmers's father, you see, he lived at the Elmses, down away by Shooter's Hill there, six or seven mile from Lunnon. He was a gentleman of spirit, and good-looking, and held his head up when he walked, and had what you may call Fire about him. He wrote poetry, and he rode, and he ran, and he cricketed, and he danced, and he acted, and he done it all equally beautiful. He was uncommon proud of Master Harry as was his only child; but he didn't spoil him, neither. He was a gentleman that had a will of his own and a eye of his own, and that would be minded. Consequently, though he made quite a companion of the fine bright boy, and was delighted to see him so fond of reading his fairy books, and was never tired of hearing him say my name is Norval, or hearing him sing his songs about Young May Moons is beaming love, and When he as adores thee has left but the name, and that:[36] still he kept the command over the child, and the child *was* a child, and it's to be wished more of 'em was!

How did Boots happen to know all this? Why, through being under-gardener. Of course he couldn't be under-gardener, and be always about, in the summertime, near the windows on the lawn, a mowing, and sweeping, and weeding, and pruning, and this and that, without getting acquainted with the ways of the family. – Even supposing Master Harry hadn't come to him one morning early, and said, 'Cobbs, how should you spell Norah, if you was asked?' and then begun cutting it in print, all over the fence.

He couldn't say he had taken particular notice of children before that; but, really it was pretty to see them two mites a going about the place together, deep in love. And the courage of the boy! Bless your soul, he'd have throwed off his little hat, and tucked up his little sleeves, and gone in at a Lion, he would, if they had happened to meet one, and she had been frightened of him. One day he stops, along with her, where Boots was hoeing weeds in the gravel, and says – speaking up, 'Cobbs,' he says, 'I like *you*.'

'Do you, sir? I'm proud to hear it.'

'Yes, I do, Cobbs. Why do I like you, do you think, Cobbs?'

'Don't know, Master Harry, I am sure.'

'Because Norah likes you, Cobbs.'

'Indeed, sir? That's very gratifying.'

'Gratifying, Cobbs? It's better than millions of the brightest diamonds, to be liked by Norah.'

'Certainly, sir.'

'You're going away, ain't you, Cobbs?'

'Yes, sir.'

'Would you like another situation, Cobbs?'

'Well, sir, I shouldn't object, if it was a good 'un.'

'Then, Cobbs,' says he, 'you shall be our Head Gardener when we are married.' And he tucks her, in her little sky-blue mantle, under his arm, and walks away.

Boots could assure me that it was better than a picter, and equal to a play, to see them babies with their long bright curling hair, their sparkling eyes, and their beautiful light tread, a rambling about the garden, deep in love. Boots was of opinion that the birds believed they was birds, and kept up with 'em, singing to please 'em. Sometimes, they would creep under the Tulip-tree, and would sit there with their arms round one another's necks, and their soft cheeks touching, a reading about the Prince, and the Dragon, and the good and bad enchanters, and the king's[37] fair daughter. Sometimes, he would hear them planning about having a house in a forest, keeping bees and a cow, and living entirely on milk and honey. Once, he came upon them by the pond, and heard Master Harry say, 'Adorable Norah, kiss me, and say you love me to distraction, or I'll jump in head-foremost.' And Boots made no question he would have done it, if she hadn't complied. On the whole, Boots said it had a tendency to make him feel as if he was in love himself – only he didn't exactly know who with.

'Cobbs,' said Master Harry one evening, when Cobbs was watering the flowers; 'I am going on a visit, this present Midsummer, to my grandmamma's at York.'

'Are you indeed, sir?' I hope you'll have a pleasant time. I am going into Yorkshire myself, when I leave here.'

'Are you going to your grandmamma's, Cobbs?'

'No, sir. I haven't got such a thing.'

'Not as a grandmamma, Cobbs?'

'No, sir.'

The boy looked on at the watering of the flowers for a little while, and then said, 'I shall be very glad indeed to go, Cobbs – Norah's going.'

'You'll be all right then, sir,' says Cobbs, 'with your beautiful sweetheart by your side.'

'Cobbs,' returned the boy, flushing, 'I never let anybody joke about it, when I can prevent them.'

'It wasn't a joke, sir,' says Cobbs with humility, 'wasn't so meant.'

'I am glad of that, Cobbs, because I like you, you know, and you're going to live with us. – Cobbs!'

'Sir.'

'What do you think my grandmamma gives me, when I go down there?'

'I couldn't so much as make a guess, sir.'

'A Bank of England five-pound note, Cobbs.'

'Whew!' says Cobbs, 'that's a spanking sum of money, Master Harry.'

'A person could do a good deal with such a sum of money as that. Couldn't a person, Cobbs?'

'I believe you, sir!'

'Cobbs,' said the boy, 'I'll tell you a secret. At Norah's house, they have been joking her about me, and pretending to laugh at our being engaged. Pretending to make game of it, Cobbs!'

'Such, sir,' says Cobbs, 'is the depravity of human natur.'

The boy, looking exactly like his father, stood for a few minutes with his glowing face towards the sunset, and then departed with 'Good-night, Cobbs. I'm going in.'

If I was to ask Boots how it happened that he was a going to leave that place just at that present time, well, he couldn't rightly answer me. He did suppose he might have stayed there till now, if he had been anyways inclined. But, you see, he was younger then and he wanted change. That's what he wanted – change. Mr Walmers, he said to him when he give him notice of his intentions to leave, 'Cobbs,' he says, 'have you anythink to complain of? I make the inquiry, because if I find that any of my people really has anything to complain of, I wish to make it right if I can.' 'No, sir,' says Cobbs; 'thanking you, sir, I find myself as well sitiwated here as I could hope to be anywheres. The truth is, sir, that I'm a going to seek my fortun.' 'O, indeed, Cobbs?' he says; 'I hope you may find it.' And Boots could assure me – which he did, touching his hair with his boot-jack, as a salute in the way of his present calling – that he hadn't found it yet.

Well, sir! Boots left the Elmses when his time was up, and Master Harry he went down to the old lady's at York, which old lady would have given that child the teeth out of her head (if she had had any), she was so wrapt up in him. What does that Infant do – for Infant you may call him and be within the mark – but cut away from that old lady's with his Norah, on a expedition to go to Gretna Green and be married!

Sir, Boots was at this identical Holly-Tree Inn (having left it several times since to better himself, but always come back through one thing or another), when, one summer afternoon the coach drives up, and out of the coach gets them two children. The Guard says to our Governor, 'I don't quite make out these little passengers, but the young gentleman's words was, that they was to be brought here.' The young gentleman gets out; hands his lady out; gives the Guard something for himself; says to our Governor, 'We're to stop here tonight, please. Sitting room and two bedrooms will be required.

Chops and cherry pudding for two!' and tucks her, in her little sky-blue mantle, under his arm, and walks into the house much bolder than Brass.

Boots leaves me to judge what the amazement of that establishment was, when those two tiny creatures all alone by themselves was marched into the Angel; – much more so, when he, who had seen them without their seeing him, give the Governor his views of the expedition they was upon. 'Cobbs,' says the Governor, 'if this is so, I must set off myself to York and quiet their friends' minds. In which case you must keep your eye upon 'em, and humour 'em, till I come back. But, before I take these measures, Cobbs, I should wish you to find from themselves whether your opinions is correct.' 'Sir to you,' says Cobbs, 'that shall be done directly.'

So, Boots goes upstairs to the Angel, and there he finds Master Harry on a enormous sofa – immense at any time, but looking like the Great Bed of Ware,[38] compared with him – a drying the eyes of Miss Norah with his pocket-hankecher. Their little legs was entirely off the ground, of course, and it really is not possible for Boots to express to me how small them children looked.

'It's Cobbs! It's Cobbs!' cries Master Harry, and comes running to him and catching hold of his hand. Miss Norah comes running to him on t'other side and catching hold of his t'other hand, and they both jump for joy.

'I see you a getting out, sir,' says Cobbs. 'I thought it was you. I thought I couldn't be mistaken in your height and figure. What's the object of your journey, sir? – Matrimonial?'

'We are going to be married, Cobbs, at Gretna Green,' returned the boy. 'We have run away on purpose. Norah has been in rather low spirits, Cobbs; but she'll be happy, now we have found you to be our friend.'

'Thank you, sir, and thank *you*, miss,' says Cobbs, 'for your good opinion. *Did* you bring any luggage with you, sir?'

If I will believe Boots when he gives me his word and honour upon it, the lady had got a parasol, a smelling bottle, a round and a half of cold buttered toast, eight peppermint drops, and a hairbrush – seemingly, a doll's. The gentleman had got about half-a-dozen yards of string, a knife, three or four sheets of writing-paper folded up surprising small, a orange, and a Chaney mug with his name upon it.

'What may be the exact natur of your plans, Sir?' says Cobbs.

'To go on,' replied the boy – which the courage of that boy was something wonderful! 'in the morning, and be married tomorrow.'

'Just so, sir,' says Cobbs. 'Would it meet your views, sir, if I was to accompany you?'

When Cobbs said this, they both jumped for joy again, and cried out, 'O yes, yes, Cobbs! Yes!'

'Well, sir,' says Cobbs. 'If you will excuse my having the freedom to give an opinion, what I should recommend would be this. I'm acquainted with a pony, sir, which, put in a phaeyton that I could borrow, would take you and Mrs Harry Walmers Junior (myself driving, if you approved), to the end of your journey in a very short space of time. I am not altogether sure, sir, that this pony will be at liberty tomorrow, but even if you had to wait over tomorrow, for him, it might be worth your while. As to the small account here, sir, in case you was to find yourself running at all short, that don't signify; because I'm a part proprietor of this inn, and it could stand over.'

Boots assures me that when they clapped their hands, and jumped for joy again, and called him 'Good Cobbs!' and 'Dear Cobbs!' and bent across him to kiss one another in the delight of their confiding hearts, he felt himself the meanest rascal for deceiving 'em, that ever was born.

'Is there anything you want just at present, sir?' says Cobbs, mortally ashamed of himself.

'We should like some cakes after dinner,' answered Master Harry, folding his arms, putting out one leg, and looking straight at him, 'and two apples – and jam. With dinner we should like to have toast-and-water. But, Norah has always been accustomed to half a glass of currant wine at dessert. And so have I.'

'It shall be ordered at the bar, sir,' says Cobbs; and away he went.

Boots has the feeling as fresh upon him at this minute of speaking, as he had then, that he would far rather have had it out in half-a-dozen rounds with the Governor, than have combined with him; and that he wished with all his heart there was any impossible place where those two babies could make an impossible marriage, and live impossibly happy ever afterwards. However, as it couldn't be, he went into the Governor's plans, and the Governor set off for York in half-an-hour.

The way in which the women of that house – without exception – every one of 'em-married *and* single – took to that boy when they heard the story, Boots considers surprising. It was as much as he could do to keep 'em from dashing into the room and kissing him. They climbed up all sorts of places, at the risk of their lives, to look at him through a pane of glass. They were seven deep at the keyhole. They was out of their minds about him and his bold spirit.

In the evening, Boots went into the room, to see how the runaway couple was getting on. The gentleman was on the window seat, supporting the lady in his arms. She had tears upon her face, and was lying, very tired and half asleep, with her head upon his shoulder.

'Mrs Harry Walmers Junior, fatigued, sir?' says Cobbs.

'Yes, she is tired, Cobbs; but, she is not used to be away from home, and she has been in low spirits again. Cobbs, do you think you could bring a biffin,[39] please?'

'I ask your pardon, sir,' says Cobbs. 'What was it you? – '

'I think a Norfolk biffin would rouse her, Cobbs. She is very fond of them.'

Boots withdrew in search of the required restorative, and, when he brought it in, the gentleman handed it to the lady, and fed her with a spoon, and took a little himself. The lady being heavy with sleep, and rather cross, 'What should you think, sir,' says Cobbs, 'of a chamber candlestick?' The gentleman approved; the chambermaid went first, up the great staircase; the lady in her sky-blue mantle, followed, gallantly escorted by the gentleman; the gentleman embraced her at her door, and retired to his own apartment, where Boots softly locked him up.

Boots couldn't but feel with increased acuteness what a base deceiver he was, when they consulted him at breakfast (they had ordered sweet milk-and-water, and toast and currant jelly, overnight), about the pony. It really was as much as he could do, he don't mind confessing to me, to look them two young things in the face, and think what a wicked old father of lies he had grown up to be. Howsomever, he went on a lying like a Trojan,[40] about the pony. He told 'em that it did so unfort'nately happen that the pony was half crippled, you see, and that he couldn't be taken out in that state, for fear it should strike to his inside. But, that he'd be finished clipped in the course of the day, and that tomorrow morning at eight o'clock the pheayton would be ready. Boots' view of the whole case, looking back upon it in my room, is, that Mrs Harry Walmers Junior was beginning to give in. She hadn't had her hair curled when she went to bed, and she didn't seem quite up to brushing it herself, and its getting in her eyes put her out. But, nothing put out Master Harry. He sat behind his breakfast cup, a tearing away at the jelly, as if he had been his own father.

After breakfast, Boots is inclined to consider that they drawed soldiers – at least, he knows that many such was found in the fireplace, all on horseback. In the course of the morning, Master Harry rang the bell – it was surprising how that there boy did carry on – and said in a sprightly way, 'Cobbs, is there any good walks in this neighborhood?'

'Yes, sir,' says Cobbs. 'There's Love Lane.'

'Get out with you, Cobbs!' – that was that there boy's expression – 'you're joking.'

'Begging your pardon, sir,' says Cobbs, 'there really is Love Lane. And a pleasant walk it is, and proud shall I be to show it to yourself and Mrs Harry Walmers Junior.'

'Norah, dear,' said Master Harry, 'this is curious. We really ought to see Love Lane. Put on your bonnet, my sweetest darling, and we will go there with Cobbs.'

Boots leaves me to judge what a Beast he felt himself to be, when that young pair told him, as they all three jogged along together, that they had made up their minds to give him two thousand guineas a year as Head Gardener, on accounts of his being so true a friend to 'em. Boots could have wished at the moment that the earth would have opened and swallowed him up; he felt so mean, with their beaming eyes a-looking at him, and believing him. Well, sir, he turned the conversation as well as he could, and he took 'em down Love Lane to the water-meadows, and there Master Harry would have drownded himself in half a moment more, a-getting out

66

a water-lily for her – but nothing daunted that boy. Well, sir, they was tired out. All being so new and strange to 'em, they was tired as tired could be. And they laid down on a bank of daisies, like the children in the wood, leastways meadows, and fell asleep.

Boots don't know – perhaps I do – but never mind, it don't signify either way – why it made a man fit to make a fool of himself, to see them two pretty babies a-lying there in the clear still sunny day, not dreaming half so hard[41] when they was asleep, as they done when they was awake. But, Lord! when you come to think of yourself, you know, and what a game you have been up to ever since you was in your own cradle, and what a poor sort of a chap you are, and how it's always either Yesterday with you, or else Tomorrow, and never Today, that's where it is!

Well, sir, they woke up at last, and then one thing was getting pretty clear to Boots: namely, that Mrs Harry Walmerses Junior's temper was on the move. When Master Harry took her round the waist, she said he 'teased her so;' and when he says, 'Norah, my young May Moon, your Harry tease you?' she tells him, 'Yes; and I want to go home!'

A biled foul, and baked bread-and-butter pudding, brought Mrs Walmers up a little; but Boots could have wished, he must privately own to me, to have seen her more sensible of the voice of love, and less abandoning of herself to currants. However, Master Harry he kept up, and his noble heart was as fond as ever. Mrs Walmers turned very sleepy about dusk, and began to cry. Therefore, Mrs Walmers went off to bed as per yesterday; and Master Harry ditto repeated.

About eleven or twelve at night, comes back the Governor in a chaise, along with Mr Walmers and a elderly lady. Mr Walmers looks amused and very serious, both at once, and says to our missis, 'We are much indebted to you, ma'am, for your kind care of our little children, which we can never sufficiently acknowledge. Pray ma'am, where is my boy?' Our missis says, 'Cobbs has the dear child in charge, sir. Cobbs, show Forty!' Then, he says to Cobbs, 'Ah Cobbs! I am glad to see *you*. I understood you was here!' And Cobbs says, 'Yes, sir. Your most obedient, sir.'

I may be surprised to hear Boots say it, perhaps; but, Boots assures me that his heart beat like a hammer, going upstairs. 'I beg your pardon, sir,' says he, while unlocking the door; 'I hope you are not angry with Master Harry. For, Master Harry is a fine boy, sir, and will do you credit and honour.' And Boots signifies to me, that if the fine boy's father had contradicted him in the daring state of mind in which he then was, he thinks he should have 'fetched him a crack,' and taken the consequences.

But, Mr Walmers only says, 'No, Cobbs. No, my good fellow. Thank you!' And, the door being opened, goes in.

Boots goes in too, holding the light, and he sees Mr Walmers go up to the bedside, bend gently down, and kiss the little sleeping face. Then, he stands looking at it for a minute, looking wonderfully like it (they do say he ran away with Mrs Walmers); and then he gently shakes the little shoulder.

'Harry, my dear boy! Harry!'

Master Harry starts up and looks at him. Looks at Cobbs too. Such is the honour of that mite, that he looks at Cobbs, to see whether he has brought him into trouble.

'I am not angry, my child. I only want you to dress yourself and come home.'

'Yes, Pa.'

Master Harry dresses himself quickly. His breast begins to swell when he has nearly finished, and it swells more and more as he stands at last, a-looking at his father; his father standing a-looking at him, the quiet image of him.

'Please may I' – the spirit of that little creatur, and the way he kept his rising tears down! – 'Please dear Pa – may I – kiss Norah, before I go?'

'You may, my child.'

So, he takes Master Harry in his hand, and Boots leads the way with the candle, and they come to that other bedroom; where the elderly lady is seated by the bed, and poor Mrs Harry Walmers Junior is fast asleep. There, the father lifts the child up to the pillow, and he lays his little face down for an instant by the little warm face of poor unconscious little Mrs Harry Walmers Junior, and gently draws it to him – a sight so touching to the chambermaids who are peeping through the door, that one of them calls out 'It's a shame to part 'em!' But this chambermaid was always, as Boots informs me, a soft-hearted one. Not that there was any harm in that girl. Far from it.

Finally, Boots says, that's all about it. Mr Walmers drove away in the chaise, having hold of Master Harry's hand. The elderly lady and Mrs Harry Walmers Junior that was never to be, (she married a Captain, long afterwards, and died in India), went off next day. In conclusion, Boots puts it to me whether I hold with him in two opinions; firstly, that there are not many couples on their way to be married, who are half as innocent of guile as those two children; secondly, that it would be a jolly good thing for a great many couples on their way to be married, if they could only be stopped in time and brought back separately.

THE LANDLORD
[by William Howitt]

Uriah Tattenhall is my elder brother by fifteen years. I am Sam Tattenhall.

My brother Uriah rang at his gate at his snug retreat of Trumpington Cottage, Peckham, near London, exactly at a quarter to six – his regular hour – when the omnibus[42] from the city set him down at the end of the lane. It was December, but the weather was fine and frosty, and as it was within a few days of Christmas, his children – four in number – two boys, just come home from school, and two girls who came home from school every day – were all on the alert to receive him, with a world of schemes for the delectation of the coming holiday time.

My brother Uriah was an especial family man. He made himself the companion and playfellow of his children on all occasions that his devotion to his business in the city would admit of. His hearty, cheery voice was heard as he entered the hall, and while he was busy pulling off his overcoat, and hanging up his hat; 'Well, my boys, well George, well Miss Lucy, there. What are you all about? How's the world used you since this morning? Where's mamma? The kettle boiling, eh?' The running fire of hilarity that always animated him seemed to throw sunshine and a new life into the house, when he came in. The children this evening rushed out into the hall, and crowded round him with such a number of 'I say, pa's and 'Do you know, pa?' and 'Don't tell him now, Mary, – let him guess. Oh! you'll never guess pa!' that he could only hurry them all into the sitting room before him like a little flock of sheep, saying, 'Well, well, you rogues – well, well, – let us have some tea, and then all about it.'

The fire blazed bonnily, as it was wont, in the bright grate, and that and the candles made the room, with light and warmth, the very paradise of comfort. Mrs Tattenhall, a handsome woman of five and thirty or so – she might be more, but she did not look it – was just in the act of pouring the water from a very bright little kettle into the equally bright silver teapot, and with a sunny, rosy, youthful, and yet matronly face, turned smilingly at his entrance, and said, 'Well, my dear, is it not a very cold night?'

'Not in this room, certainly, my dear,' said my brother Uriah, 'and with such a snuggery before one, who cares for cold outside.'

Mrs Tattenhall gave him a brighter smile still, and the neat Harriet coming in with the toast, the whole family group was speedily seated round the tea table, and the whole flood of anticipated pleasures and plans of the younger population let loose, and cordially entered into, and widened and improved by my brother Uriah. He promised them an early night at the very best pantomime, and they were to read all about all the pantomimes in the newspapers, and find out which was the best. He meant to take them to see all sorts of sights, and right off-hand on Christmas Eve he was going to set up a Christmas tree, and have Christkindchen,[43] and all sorts of gifts under it for everybody. He had got it all ready done by a German who came often to his warehouse, and it was somewhere, not far off just now.

'Thank you, papa, – thank you a thousand times. Oh! what heaps of fun!' exclaimed the children, altogether.

'Why, really, my dear,' said Mrs Tattenhall, delighted as the children, 'what has come to you? You quite out-do yourself, good as you always are. You are quite magnificent in your projects.'

'To be sure,' said Uriah, taking hold of the hands of little Lucy, and dancing round the room with her. 'To be sure; we may just as well be merry as sad; it will be all the same a hundred years hence.'

Presently the tea table was cleared, and, as they drew round the fire, my brother Uriah pulled out a book, and said, 'George, there's a nice book – begin, and read it aloud: it will be a very pleasant book for these winter evenings before all the dissipation begins. It is Pringle's *Adventures in South Africa*, and is almost as good as *Robinson Crusoe*.[44] I knew Pringle well; a lame, little man, that you never would dream could sit on a horse, much less ride after lions and elephants in that style.'

'Lions and elephants!' all were silent, and George read on. He read till eight o'clock, their bedtime, and the whole group – parents and children – were equally delighted with it. As they closed the book – 'Now,' said the father, 'would it not be grand fun to live out there, and ride after the lions and elephants?'

'Ah! grand fun!' said the boys, but the mother and the girls shuddered at the lions.

'Well, you could stay in the house, you know,' said Bob.

'Right, my fine fellow,' said the father, clapping him on the shoulder. 'So now off to bed, and dream all about it.'

When the children were gone my brother Uriah stretched out his feet on the fender and fell into a silence. When my brother's silence had lasted some time his wife said, 'Are you sleepy, my dear?'

'No; never was more wakeful,' said Uriah; 'really, my dear, I never was less inclined to be sprightly: but it won't do to dash the spirits of the children. Let them enjoy the Christmas as much as they can, they will never be young but once.'

'What is amiss?' asked Mrs Tattenhall, with a quick apprehensive look. 'Is there something amiss? Good gracious! you frighten me.'

'Why no, there is nothing exactly amiss; there is nothing new; but the fact is, I have just taken stock, and today finished casting all up, and struck the balance.'

'And is it bad? Is it less than you expected?' asked Mrs Tattenhall, fixing her eyes seriously on her husband's face.

'Bad? No, not bad, nor good. I'll tell you what it is. You've heard of a toad in a mud wall.[45] Well, that's me. Twenty years ago, I went into business with exactly three thousand pounds, and here I have been trading, and fagging, and caring, and getting, and losing, business extending, and profits getting less and less, making large sales, and men breaking directly after, and so the upshot is, – twenty years trade, and the balance the same to a pound as that I began with. Three thousand I started with, and three thousand is precisely my capital at this moment.'

'Is that all?' said Mrs Tattenhall, wonderfully relieved. 'Be thankful, my dear Uriah, that you have three thousand pounds. You have your health wonderfully, we have all our health; we have children, as good and promising children as anybody is blest with, and a happy home, and live as well and comfortably as any one need to do, or as I wish, I am sure. What do we want more?'

'What do we want more?' said Uriah, drawing up his legs suddenly, and clapping his hands in a positive sort of a way on his knees. 'Why, I for one, want a great deal more. We've children, you say, and a home, and all that. Heaven be thanked, so we have! but I want our children to have a home after us. Three thousand pounds divided amongst four, leaves about seven hundred and fifty each. Is it worthwhile to fag a whole life, and leave them that and a like prospect? No,' continued Uriah, in a considering manner, and shaking his head. 'No, I want something more; more for myself; more for them; more room, more scope, a wider horizon, and a more proportionate result of a whole human existence. And do you know Maria what I have come to as the best conclusion? To go out to Australia.'

'To go out to Australia!' said Mrs Tattenhall, in astonishment. 'My dear Uriah, you are joking. You mean no such thing.'

'But that is just what I do mean,' said Uriah, taking his wife's hand affectionately; 'I have thought of it long, and the toad-in-the-wall balance has determined me. And now what I ask of you is to look at it calmly and earnestly. You know the Smiths, the Browns, and the Robinsons have gone out. They report the climate delicious, and that wonders are doing. A new country, if it be a good country, is the place to grow and thrive in, without doubt. Look at the trees in a wood. They grow up and look very fine in the mass. The wood, you say, is a very fine wood; but when you have looked at the individual trees, they are crowded and spindled up. They cannot put out a single bough beyond a certain distance; if they attempt it, their presuming twigs are poked back again by sturdy neighbours all round, that are all struggling for light and space like them. Look then at the tree on the open plain, – how it spreads and hangs in grand amplitude its unobstructed boughs and foliage: a lordly object. Just so, this London. It is a vast, a glorious, a most imposing London, but thousands of its individuals in it are pressed and circumscribed to a few square yards and not more. Give me the open plain, – the new country, and then see if I do not put out a better head, and our children too.'

Mrs Tattenhall, now she felt that her husband was in earnest, sat motionless and confounded. The shock had come too suddenly upon her. Her husband, it is true, had often told her that things did not move as he wished; that they seemed fixed, and stereotyped, and stagnant; but then, when *are* merchants satisfied? She never had entertained an idea but that they should go on to the end of the chapter as they had been going on ever since she was married. She was bound up heart and soul with her own country; she had her many friends and relations, with whom she lived on the most cordial terms; all her tastes, feelings, and ideas were English and metropolitan. At the very idea of quitting England, and for so new, and so distant a country, she was seized with an indescribable consternation

'My dear Maria!' said her husband; 'mind, I don't ask you to go at first. You and the children can remain here till I have been and seen what the place and prospects are like. My brother Sam will look after business – he will soon be at home in it – and if all is pleasant, why, you will come then, if not I won't ask you. I'll work out a good round sum myself if possible, or open up some connection that will mend matters here. What can I say more?'

'Nothing, dear Uriah, nothing. But those poor children – '

'Those poor children!' said Uriah. 'Why my dear Maria, if you were to ask them whether they would like a voyage to Australia, to go and see those evergreen woods, and gallop about all amongst gay parrots, and great kangaroos, they would jump off their seats with joy. The spirits of the young are ever on the wing for adventure and new countries. It is the prompting of that Great Power which has constructed all this marvellous universe, and bade mankind multiply and replenish the earth. Don't trouble yourself about them. You saw how they devoured the adventures at the Cape, and you'll see how they will kindle up in a wonderful enthusiasm at the promise of a voyage to Australia. What are pantomimes to that?'

'Poor things!' said Mrs Tattenhall. 'They know nothing about the reality; all is fairyland and poetry to them.'

'The reality! the reality, Maria, will be all fairyland and poetry to them.'

Mrs Tattenhall shook her head, and retired that night – not to sleep, but with a very sad heart to ruminate over this unexpected revelation. My brother's words were realised at the first mention of the project to the children. After the first shock of surprise and doubt whether it were really meant, they became unboundedly delighted. The end of it was, that by the middle of February, my brother Uriah, having had a handsome offer for his business and stock, had wound up all his affairs; and Mrs Tattenhall having concluded, like a good wife and mother, to go with the whole family, they bade farewell to England, Mrs Tattenhall with many tears, Uriah serious and thoughtful, the children full of delight and wonder at everything in the ship.

They had a fine voyage, though with very few passengers, for the captain said there was a temporary damp on the Australian colonies. The order of the Government at home to raise the upset price of land to one pound per acre, had checked emigration, and as there had been a good deal of speculation in Melbourne in town allotments, things just now looked gloomy. This was in eighteen hundred and forty-three. 'But it can't last long,' said the Captain, 'that silly order of raising the price of the land is so palpably absurd; while America is selling land so much nearer at a quarter of the price, that it must be repealed; and then all will be right again.'

It was the middle of May when our party arrived in Hobson's Bay. It was very rainy, gloomy weather – the very opposite to all that the climate had been represented in the accounts sent home – but then it was the commencement of winter, the November of our season. Uriah got a boat, and sailed up the winding river to the town. The sail was through a flat tract of land densely overgrown with a mass of close, dark bushes, of some ten feet high, somewhat resembling our sloe-tree,[46] the tea-tree of that country. On reaching the foot of the town, which stood on a range of low hills, Uriah and his companions stepped out into a most appalling slough of black mud, through which they waded till they reached the town, which was of no great extent, scattered over a considerable space, however, for the number of houses, and with great intervals of woodland, and of places where the trees had been felled, and where the stumps, a yard high, remained in unsightly nakedness.

Uriah walked on through a scene which, somehow in keeping with the weather, fell heavily on his spirits. There was nothing doing, or stirring; houses in various degrees of progress stood as they were. There were piles of timber, lime, shingles, posts, and rails, empty wagons and carts, but no people employed about them. On every hand he saw lots marked out for fencing or building upon, but there they remained all stationary.

'Is it Sunday?' Uriah asked himself. No, it was Tuesday. Then why all this stagnation; this solitude? In a lane, or rather deep track of mud and ruts, since known as Finder's Lane, but then without a name, and only just wide enough between the trees for a cart to pass, Uriah wading and plunging along, the rain meantime pouring, streaming, and drumming down on his umbrella, he came face to face with a large active man in a mackintosh[47] cloak, and an oilskin hood over his head. Neither of them found it very convenient to step out of the middle mud track, because on each side of it rose a perfect bank of sludge raised by the wheels of drays, and stopping to have a look at each other, the strange man suddenly put out a huge red hand warm and wet, and exclaimed:

'What! Tattenhall! You here! In the name of all wonders what could bring you here at this moment?'

'What, Robinson! is that you?' cried Uriah. 'Is this your climate? This your paradise?'

'Climate – paradise – be hanged!' said Robinson. 'They're well enough. If everything else were as well there would be nought to complain of. But tell me Uriah Tattenhall, with that comfortable Trumpington Cottage at Peckham, with that well-to-do warehouse in the Old Jewry, what could possess you to come here?'

'What should I come for, but to settle?' asked Uriah, somewhat chagrined at this salutation.

'To settle! ha, ha!' burst out Robinson. 'Well, as for that, you could not come to a better place. It is a regular settler here. Everything and everybody are settled here out and out. This is a settlement, and no mistake; but it is like a many other settlements, the figures are all on the wrong side the ledger.'

'Good gracious!' said Uriah.

'Nay, it is neither good nor gracious,' replied Robinson. 'Look round. What do you see? Ruin, desertion, dirt, and the – devil!'

'Why, how is that?' asked Uriah. 'I thought you, and Jones, and Brown, and all of you had made your fortunes.'

'So we had, or were just on the point of doing. We had purchased lots of land for building, and had sold it out again at five hundred per cent, when chop! down come little Lord John with his pound an acre,[48] and heigh, presto! everything goes topsy turvy. Our purchasers are either in the bankruptcy court, or have vanished. By jingo! I could show you such lots, fine lots for houses and gardens, for shops and warehouses; ay, and shops and warehouses upon them too, as would astonish you.'

'Well, and what then?' asked Uriah.

'What then! why man don't you comprehend. Emigration is stopped, broken off as short as a pipe-shank, not a soul is coming out to buy and live in all these houses – not a soul except an old – excuse me, Tattenhall, I was going to say, except you and another fool or two. But where do you hang out? Look! there is my house,' pointing to a wooden erection near. 'I'll come and see you as soon as I know where you fix yourself.'

'But mind one thing,' cried Uriah, seizing him by the arm as he passed. 'For heaven's sake, don't talk in this manner to my wife. It would kill her.'

'Oh no, mum's the word! There's no use frightening the woman,' said Robinson. 'No, confound it. I won't croak anyhow. And, after all, bad as things are, why, they can't remain so forever. Nothing ever does, that's one comfort. They'll mend sometime.'

'When?' said Uriah.

'Well,' said Robinson, pausing a little, 'not before you and I meet again, so I may leave that answer to another opportunity;' and with a nod and very knowing look he stalked on.

'Odd fellow,' said my brother Uriah. 'He is very jocose for a ruined man. What is one to think?' and he waded on. After making a considerable circuit, and actually losing himself in the woods somewhere about where the Reverend Mr Morrison's chapel now stands in Collin's Street, he again came across Robinson who stood at the door of a considerable erection of wattle-and-dab, that is, a building of boughs wattled on stakes, and dabbed over with mud; then not uncommon in Melbourne, and still common enough in the bush. It stood on the hillside with a swift muddy torrent produced by the rains rushing down the valley below it, towards the river, as it had often done since it bore the name of Swanston Street.

'Here, Tattenhall! here is a pretty go!' shouted Robinson; 'a fellow has cut with bag and baggage tonight who owes me four thousand pounds, and has left me a lot more houses and land. That's the way every day. But look, here is a house ready for you. You can't have a better, and you can pay me any trifle you like, something is better than nothing.'

He led Uriah in. The house was thoroughly and comfortably furnished; though, of course, very simply, with beds and everything. Uriah in less than a week, was safely established there, and had time to ramble about with his boys, and learn more fully the condition of the colony. It was melancholy beyond description. Wild, reckless speculation brought to a sudden close by the cessation of immigration, had gone like a hurricane over the place, and had left nothing but ruin and paralysis behind it. No words that Robinson had used, or that any man could use, could overpaint the real condition of prostration and of misery. Two hundred and eight insolvencies in a population of ten thousand, told the tale of awful reality. Uriah was overwhelmed with consternation at the step he had taken. O! how pleasant seemed that Trumpington Cottage, Peckham, and that comfortable warehouse in the Old Jewry, as he viewed them from the Antipodes in the midst of rain and ruin.

What, however, was my brother Uriah's astonishment to see Robinson stalk in the next day, his tall figure having to stoop at every door, and in his brusque, noisy way, go up to Mrs Tattenhall, and shaking her hand as you would shake the handle of a pump, congratulate her on her arrival in the colony.

'A lucky hit, madam, a most lucky, scientific hit! Ah! trust Tattenhall for knowing what he is about.'

Mrs Tattenhall stood with a singular expression of wonder and bewilderment on her countenance, for the condition of the place, and the condolings of several female neighbours who had dropped in in Uriah's absence, had induced her to believe that they had made a fatal move of it.

'Why, sir,' said she, 'what can you mean, for as I hear, the place is utterly ruined, and certainly it looks like it?'

'Ruined! to be sure it is, at least the people are, more's the pity for me, and the like of me who have lost everything; but for Tattenhall who has everything to gain, and money to win it with, why it is the golden opportunity, the very thing! If he had watched at all the four corners of the world, and for a hundred years, he could not have dropped into such a chance. Ah! trust Tattenhall, make me believe he did not plan it.' Thrusting his knuckles into Uriah's side, and laughing with a thunderclap of a laugh that seemed to come from lungs of leather.

'Why, look here now,' he continued, drawing a chair and seating himself on its front edge; 'look here now, if you had come six months ago, you could have bought nothing except out of the fire. Town allotments, land, houses, bread, meat, sugar, everything ten times the natural price; and, now! cheap, dog cheap? of no value at all, you might have them for asking for; nay, I could go into a dozen deserted shops and take any quantity for nothing. And property? why three thousand pounds cash would almost buy all the place – all the colony.'

'What is the use,' asked Mrs Tattenhall, 'of buying a ruined colony?'

'A ruined colony!' said Robinson, edging himself still more forward in his chair, and seeming actually to sit upon nothing, his huge figure and large ruddy face appearing still larger. 'The colony, madam, is not ruined; never was ruined, never can be ruined. The people are ruined, a good lot of them; but the colony is a good and a grand colony. God made the colony, and let me tell you, madam,' looking very serious, 'Providence is no speculator, up today, down tomorrow. What he does he does. Well, the people have ruined themselves; but it is out of their power to ruin the colony; no, nor the town. The town and the colony are sound as a bell, never were sounder, never had more stuff in them; never had so much. There is the land still, not a yard of it has gone; no great fellow has put that on his back and gone off with it. The land is there, and the houses, and the merchandise, and the flocks, and herds, and horses: and – what concerns you – '

He sate and looked at Mrs Tattenhall, who stood there intently listening, and Uriah stood just behind her listening too, and all the children with their mouths open, gazing on the strange man.

'Well, what – what concerns us?' said Mrs Tattenhall.

'To get a huge, almighty heap of something for nothing,' said the large man, stretching out his arms in a circular shape, as if he would enclose a whole globe, and in a low, slow, deep tone, calculated to sink deep into the imaginations of the listeners.

'If we did but know when things would mend;' said my brother Uriah, for the first time venturing to put in a word.

'When!' said Robinson starting up so suddenly that his head struck against a beam in the low one-storeyed house. 'Confound these low places,' said he, turning fiery red, and rubbing his crown, 'there will be better anon. When? say ye?

Hark ye! this colony is – how old? Eight years! and in eight years what a town! what wealth! what buildings! what a power of sheep and cattle! The place is knocked down, won't it get up again? Ay, and quickly! Here are a pair of sturdy legs,' he said, turning to Bob, who flushed up in surprise; 'but, Mrs Tattenhall, you did not teach him to walk without a few tumbles, eh? But he got up again, and how he stands now! what a sturdy young rogue it is! And what made him get up again? Because he was young and strong, and the colony is young and strong, madam. Eight years old! What shall I give you for a three thousand pounds purchase made now, three years hence? Just think of that,' said the tall man, 'just turn that over a time or two,' nodding solemnly to my brother, and then to my sister-in-law, and then cautiously glancing at the menacing beam, and with a low duck diving out of the house.

'What a strange fellow!' said Uriah.

'But how true!' said Mrs Tattenhall.

'How true! What true?' asked Uriah, astonished.

'Why,' said Mrs Tattenhall, 'what he says. It is truth, Uriah; we must buy as much as we can.'

'But,' said Uriah, 'only the other day he said the clean contrary. He said everybody was ruined.'

'And he says so still,' added Mrs Tattenhall, enthusiastically, 'but not the colony. We must buy! We must buy, and wait. One day we shall reap a grand harvest.'

'Ah!' said Uriah; 'so you let yourself, my dear Maria, be thus easily persuaded, because Robinson wants to sell, and thinks we have money?'

'Is it not common sense, however? Is it not the plainest sense?' asked Mrs Tattenhall. 'Do you think this colony is never to recover?'

'Never is a long while,' said Uriah. 'But still – '

'Well, we will think it over, and see how the town lies; and where the chief points of it will be, probably, hereafter; and if this Mr Robinson has any land in such places, I would buy of him, because he has given us the first idea of it.'

They thought and looked, and the end of it was, that very soon they had bought up land and houses, chiefly from Robinson, to the amount of two thousand pounds. Robinson fain would not have sold, but have mortgaged; and that fact was the most convincing proof hat he was sincere in his expectations of a revival. Time went on. Things were more and more hopeless. Uriah, who had nothing else to do, set on and cultivated a garden. He had plenty of garden ground, and his boys helped him, and enjoyed it vastly. As the summer went on, and melons grew ripe, and there were plenty of green peas and vegetables, by the addition of meat, which was now only one penny a-pound, they could live almost for nothing; and Uriah thought they could wait and maintain themselves for years, if necessary. So from time to time, one tale of urgent staring distress or another lured him on to take fresh bargains, till he saw himself almost penniless. Things still remained as dead as the very stones or the stumps around them. My brother Uriah began to feel very melancholy; and Mrs Tattenhall, who had so strongly advised the wholesale purchase of property, looked very serious. Uriah often thought: 'Ah she *would* do it; but – Bless her! I will never say so, for she did it for the best.' But his boys and girls, were growing apace, and made him think. 'Bless me! In a few years they will be shooting up into men and women; and if this speculation should turn out all moonshine! – if the place should never revive!'

He sate one day on the stump of a tree on a high ground, looking over the bay. His mind was in the most gloomy, dejected condition. Everything looked dark and hopeless. No evidence of returning life around; no spring in the commercial world; and his good money gone; as he sate thus, his eyes fixed on the distance, his mind sunk in the lowering present, a man came up, and asked him to take his land off his hands: to take it, for Heaven's sake, and save his starving family.

'Man!' said Uriah, with a face and a voice so savage that it made the suppliant start, even in his misery. 'I have no money! I want no land! I have too much land. You shall have it all for as much as will carry me back to England, and set me down a beggar there.'

The man shook his head. 'If I had a single crown I would not ask you; but my wife is down of the fever, and my children are dying of dysentery. What shall I do? and my lots are the very best in the place.'

'I tell you!' said my brother Uriah, with a fierce growl, and an angry flash of the eye, 'I have no money, and how can I buy?'

He glanced at the man in fury; but a face so full of patient suffering and of sickness – sickness of the heart, of the soul, and, as it were, of famine, met his gaze, that he stopped short, felt a pang of remorse for his anger, and, pointing to a number of bullocks grazing in the valley below, he said, in a softened tone, 'Look there! The other day a man told me such a tale of horror – a sick family, and a goal staring him in the face, that I gave him my last money – my carefully hoarded money, and of what use are those cattle to me? None whatever: You may have them for your land, if you like. I have nothing else.'

'I will have them,' said the man. 'On a distant station I know where I could sell them, if I could only leave my family. But they have no flour, no tea, nothing but meat, meat, meat.'

'Leave them to me,' said Uriah, feeling the warm blood and the spirit of humanity beginning to circulate in his bosom at the sense of what was really suffering around him. 'Leave them to me. I will care for them. Your wife and children shall have a doctor. I will find you some provisions for your journey, and if ever your land is worth anything, you shall have it again. This state of things makes monsters of us. It turns our blood into gall, our hearts into stones. We must resist it, or we are ruined, indeed!'

'Nay,' said the man, 'I won't impose upon you. Take that piece of land in the valley there; it will one day be valuable.'

'That!' said Uriah, looking. 'That! Why, that is a swamp! I will take that – I shall not hurt you there!' And he laughed outright, the first time for two years.

Years went on, and my brother Uriah lived on, but as it were in the valley of the shadow of death.[49] It was a melancholy and dispiriting time. The buoyancy of his soul was gone. That jovial, sunny ebullient spirit with which he used to come home from the city, in England, had fled, as a thing that had never been. He maintained himself chiefly out of his garden. His children were springing up into long, lanky lads and lasses. He educated them himself, as well as he could; and as for clothes! Not a navvy – not a beggar – in the streets of London, but could have stood a comparison with them, to their infinite disparagement. Ah! those good three thousand pounds! How will the balance stand in my brother Uriah's books at the end of the next twenty years?

But anon there awoke a slight motion in the atmosphere of life. It was a mere flutter of the air, that died out again. Then again it revived – it strengthened – it blew like a breath of life over the whole landscape. Uriah looked around him from the very place where he had sat on the stump in despair. It was bright and sunny. He heard a sound of an axe and a hammer. He looked, and saw a house, that had stood a mere skeleton, once more in progress. There were people passing to and fro with a more active air. What is that? A cart of goods? A dray of building materials. There was life and motion again! The discovery of converting sheep and oxen into tallow had raised the value of stock. The shops and merchants were once more in action. The man to whom he had sold the oxen came up smiling –

'Things mend, sir. We shall soon be all right. And that piece of land in the swamp, that you were so merry over, will you sell it? It lies near the wharves, and is wanted for warehouses.'

'Bravo!' cried Uriah, and they descended the hill together. Part of the land was sold; and soon substantial warehouses of the native trapstone,[50] were rising upon it. Uriah's old attachment to a merchant's life came over him. With the purchase money he built a warehouse too. Labour was extremely low, and he built a large and commodious one.

Another year or two, and behold Uriah busy in his warehouse; his two boys clerking it gravely in the counting-house. Things grew rapidly better. Uriah and his family were once more handsomely clad, handsomely housed, and Uriah's jolly humour was again in the ascendant. Every now and then Robinson came hurrying in, a very busy man, indeed he was now, in the town council, and moreover, mayor; and saying, 'Well, Mrs Tattenhall, didn't I say it, eh? Is not this boy of a colony on a fine sturdy pair of legs again? Not down? Not dead? Well, well! Tattenhall did me a kindness, then – by ready cash for my land – I don't forget it; but I don't know how I am to make him amends, unless I come and dine with him some day.' And he was off again.

Another year or two, and that wonderful crisis, the gold discovery, came. Then, what a sensation – what a stir – what a revolution, what running, and buying and bidding for land, for prime business situations! – what rolling in of people – capital – goods. Heaven and earth! – what a scene – what a place – what a people.

Ten years to a day from the last balance at the Old Jewry, Uriah Tattenhall balanced again, and his three thousand pounds, was grown to seventy thousand pounds, and was still rolling up and on like a snowball.

There were George and Bob grown into really tall and handsome fellows. George was the able merchant. Bob had got a station out at the Dundenong-Hills, and told wonderful stories of riding after kangaroos, and wild bulls, and shooting splendid lyre-birds – all of which come in reading Pringle's *Life in South Africa*. There were Mary and Lucy, two handsome girls as any in the colony, and wonderfully attractive to a young Benson and a younger Robinson. Wonders were the next year to bring forth, and amongst them was to be a grand picnic at Bob's station, at the Dundenong, in which they were to live out in real tents in the forest, and cook, and bake, and brew, and the ladies were to join in a bull-hunt, and shoot with revolvers, and nobody was to be hurt, or thrown, or anything to happen, but all sorts of merriment and wildwood life.

And really my brother's villa on the Yarra River is a very fine place. The house is an Italian villa built of real stone, ample, with large, airy rooms, a broad verandah, and all in the purest taste. It stands on a high bank above the valley, in which the Yarra winds, taking a sweep there, its course marked by a dense body of acacia trees. In the spring these trees are of resplendent gold, loading the air with their perfume. Now they were thick and dark in their foliage, casting their shade on the river deep between its banks. From the house the view presented this deep valley with this curving track of trees, and beyond slopes divided into little farms, with their little homesteads upon them, where Uriah had a number of tenants making their fortunes on some thirty or forty acres each, by hay at forty pounds a ton, and potatoes and onions at one shilling a pound, and all other produce in proportion.

On this side of the river you saw extensive gardens in the hollow blooming with roses and many tropical flowers, and along the hillsides on either hand vineyards and fruit orchards of the most vigorous vegetation, and loaded with young fruit. The party assembled at my brother Uriah's house on that hospitable Christmas day, descended amid a native shrubbery, and Uriah thrust a walking stick to its very handle into the rich black soil, and when his friends expressed their surprise, he told them that the soil there was fourteen feet deep, and would grow any quantity of produce for ages without manuring. Indeed, they passed through green corn of the most luxuriant character, and, crossing the bridge of a brook which there fell into the river, they found themselves under the acacias; by the river side there lay huge prostrate trunks of ancient gum-trees,[51] the patriarchs of the forest, which had fallen and given place to the acacia, and now reminded the spectators that they were still in the land of primitive woods.

'Why, Tattenhall,' said Robinson, to my brother Uriah, 'Trumpington Cottage, my dear fellow, would cut a poor figure after this. I'd ask any lord or gentleman to show me a fertiler or more desirable place in the tight little island. Bigger houses there may be, and are, but not to my mind more desirable. Do you know, very large houses always seem to me a sort of asylums for supernumerary servants – the master can only occupy a corner there – he cuts out quite small in the bulk. And as to fertility, this beats Battersea Fields and Fulham hollow. Those market gardeners might plant and plant to all eternity, always taking out and never putting in, and if they could grow peaches, apricots, grapes, figs, twice a year, and all that as fine in the open air as they do in hothouses, and sell their bunches of parsley at sixpence apiece, and watermelons – gathered from any gravel heap or dry open field – at five shillings apiece, plentiful as pumpkins, wouldn't they astonish themselves!

'But what makes you call this place Bowstead?' continued Robinson, breaking off a small wattle-bough[52] to whisk the flies from his face. 'Orr has named his Abbotsford – that's because he's a Scotchman; and we've got Cremorne Gardens, and Richmond, and Hawthorne, and all sorts of English names about here; – but Bowstead! I can't make it out.'

'You can't?' said Uriah, smiling; 'don't you see that the river curves in a bow here, and stead is a place?'

'O! that's it,' said Robinson; 'I fancied it was to remind you of Bow Bells.'

'There you have it,' said Bob, laughing. 'Bow Bells! but, as there was a bow and no bells, my father put a stead to it, that's instead of the bells, you know.'

'Bless me!' said Robinson: 'now I should never have thought of that – how very clever.'

And he took the joke in such perfect simplicity, that all burst into a simultaneous laugh; for every one else knew that it was so called in honour of Maria Bowstead, now the universally respected Mrs Tattenhall.

The whole party were very merry, for they had good cause to be. Mr and Mrs Tattenhall, still in their prime, spread out, enlarged every way, in body and estate, rosy, handsomely dressed, saw around them nothing but prosperity. A paradise of their own, in which they saw their children already developed into that manly and feminine beauty so conspicuous in our kindred of the south; their children already taking root in the land and twining their branches amongst those of other opulent families, they felt the full truth of Robinson's rude salutation, as he exclaimed, on coming to a fresh and more striking view of the house and grounds, –

'Ah! Tattenhall, Tattenhall!' giving him one of his jocose pokes in the side, 'didn't I say you knew very well what you were about when you came here, eh? Mrs Tattenhall, ma'am? Who said it? Robinson, wasn't it, eh?'

When they returned to the house, and had taken tea in a large tent on the lawn, and the young people had played a lively game of romps or bo-peep amongst the bushes of the shrubbery, with much laughter, the great drawing room was lighted up, and very soon there was heard the sounds of violins and dancing feet. My brother Uriah and his wife were at that moment sitting under the verandah, enjoying the fresh evening air, the scent of tropical trees and flowers which stole silently through the twilight, and the clear, deep blue of the sky, where the magnificent constellations of Orion and the Scorpion were growing momentarily into their full nocturnal splendour. As the music broke out my brother Uriah affectionately pressed the hand of his wife, faithful and wise and encouraging through the times of their difficulty and depression, and saying 'Thank God for all this!' the pressure was as affectionately and grate-fully returned. Then my brother and his wife rose up, and passed into the blaze of light which surrounded the gay and youthful company within.

THE BARMAID
[by Adelaide Anne Procter]

She was a pretty, gentle girl – a farmer's orphan daughter, and the landlord's niece – whom I strongly suspected of being engaged to be married very shortly, to the writer of the letter that I saw her reading at least twenty times, when I passed the bar, and which I more than believe I saw her kiss one night. She told me a tale of that country which went so pleasantly to the music of her voice, that I ought rather to say it turned itself into verse, than was turned into verse by me.

A little past the village
    The sun stood, low and white,
Green shady trees behind it,
    And an orchard on the right,
Where over the green paling
    The red-cheeked apples hung,
As if to watch how wearily
    The sign-board creaked and swung.

The heavy-laden branches
    Over the road hung low,
Reflecting fruit or blossom
    In the wayside well below;
Where children, drawing water,
    Looked up and paused to see,
Amid the apple branches,
    A purple Judas Tree.[53]

The road stretch'd winding onward
　　For many a weary mile–
So dusty footsore wanderers
　　Would pause and rest awhile;
And panting horses halted,
　　And travellers loved to tell
The quiet of the wayside inn,
　　The orchard, and the well.

Here Maurice dwelt; and often
　　The sunburnt boy would stand
Gazing upon the distance,
　　And shading with his hand
His eyes, while watching vainly
　　For travellers, who might need
His aid to loose the bridle,
　　And tend the weary steed.

And once (the boy remember'd
　　That morning many a day –
The dew lay on the hawthorn,
　　The bird sang on the spray)
A train of horsemen, nobler
　　Than he had seen before,
Up from the distance gallopp'd
　　And paused before the door.

Upon a milk-white pony,
　　Fit for a faery queen,
Was the loveliest little damsel
　　His eyes had ever seen;

A servant-man was holding
  The leading rein, to guide
The pony and its mistress
  Who cantered by his side.

Her sunny ringlets round her
  A golden cloud had made,
While her large hat was keeping
  Her calm blue eyes in shade;
One hand held firm the silken reins
  To keep her steed in check,
The other pulled his tangled mane,
  Or stroked his glossy neck.

And as the boy brought water,
  And loosed the rein, he heard
The sweetest voice, that thank'd him
  In one low gentle word;
She turned her blue eyes from him,
  Look'd up, and smiled to see
The hanging purple blossoms
  Upon the Judas Tree.

And show'd it with a gesture,
  Half pleading, half command,
Till he broke the fairest blossom,
  And laid it in her hand;
And she tied it to her saddle
  With a ribbon from her hair,
While her happy laugh rang gaily,
  Like silver on the air.

But the champing steeds were rested–
    The horsemen now spurr'd on,
And down the dusty highway
    They vanish'd and were gone.
Years pass'd, and many a traveller
    Paused at the old inn-door,
But the little milk-white pony
    And the child return'd no more.

Years pass'd, the apple branches
    A deeper shadow shed;
And many a time the Judas Tree,
    Blossom and leaf lay dead;
When on the loitering western breeze
    Came the bells' merry sound,
And flowery arches rose, and flags
    And banners waved around.

And Maurice stood expectant,
    The bridal train would stay
Some moments at the inn-door,
    The eager watchers say;
They come – the cloud of dust draws near–
    'Mid all the state and pride,
He only sees the golden hair
    And blue eyes of the bride.

The same, yet, ah! still fairer,
    He knew the face once more
That bent above the pony's neck
    Years past at the inn-door:

Her shy and smiling eyes look'd round,
　Unconscious of the place –
Unconscious of the eager gaze
　He fix'd upon her face.

He pluck'd a blossom from the tree–
　The Judas Tree – and cast
Its purple fragrance towards the bride,
　A message from the Past.
The signal came, the horses plunged–
　Once more she smiled around;
The purple blossom in the dust
　Lay trampled on the ground.

Again the slow years fleeted,
　Their passage only known
By the height the Passion-flower
　Around the porch had grown:
And many a passing traveller
　Paused at the old inn-door,
But the bride, so fair and blooming
　Return'd there never more.

One winter morning, Maurice,
　Watching the branches bare,
Rustling and waving dimly
　In the gray and misty air,
Saw blazon'd on a carriage
　Once more the well-known shield,
The azure fleurs-de-lis and stars
　Upon a silver field.

He looked – was that pale woman,
  So grave, so worn, so sad,
The child, once young and smiling,
  The bride, once fair, and glad?
What grief had dimm'd that glory
  And brought that dark eclipse
Upon her blue eyes' radiance,
  And paled those trembling lips?

What memory of past sorrow,
  What stab of present pain,
Brought that deep look of anguish,
  That watch'd the dismal rain,
That watch'd (with the absent spirit
  That looks, yet does not see)
The dead and leafless branches
  Upon the Judas Tree.

The slow dark months crept onward
  Upon their icy way,
'Till April broke in showers,
  And Spring smiled forth in May,
Upon the apple-blossoms
  The sun shone bright again,
When slowly up the highway
  Came a long funeral train.

The bells toll'd slowly, sadly,
  For a noble spirit fled;
Slowly, in pomp and honour.
  They bore the quiet dead.

Upon a black-plumed charger
    One rode, who held a shield,
Where azure fleurs-de-lis and stars
    Shone on a silver field.

'Mid all that homage given
    To a fluttering heart at rest,
Perhaps an honest sorrow
    Dwelt only in one breast.
One by the inn-door standing
    Watch'd with fast-dropping tears
The long procession passing,
    And thought of bygone years.

The boyish, silent homage
    To child and bride unknown,
The pitying tender sorrow
    Kept in his heart alone,
Now laid upon the coffin,
    With a purple flower, might be
Told to the cold dead sleeper;
    The rest could only see
A fragrant purple blossom
    Pluck'd from a Judas Tree.

THE POOR PENSIONER
[by Harriet Parr]

I met her in the corridor, walking to and fro, and muttering to herself with a down-looking aspect, and a severe economy of dress, the season considered. I wondered how she came there, and was, to say the least of it, decidedly startled when she stopped directly opposite me, and, lifting a pair of blank, brown eyes to my face, said, in a stern voice:

'He was not guilty, my lord judge. God will right him yet. It will all come out some day. I can wait: yes, I can wait. I am more patient than death. I am more patient than injustice.'

I made a hasty and undignified retreat downstairs when she left the passage free, and, meeting the waiter, inquired who the woman was. The man touched his forehead significantly, and said that she was harmless (I was very glad to hear it); and that she lived on the broken victuals; and that his mistress always gave her a dinner on Christmas day. While we were speaking together, she descended to where we stood, and repeated the exact formula of which she had made use before. She was a tall woman, strong-limbed, and thin to meagerness. She might be fifty or perhaps fifty-five; her skin was withered, and tanned by exposure to all sorts of weather, and her uncovered hair was burnt to a rusty iron-grey. The waiter suggested to her to go to the kitchen fire; at which she broke into a scornful laugh, and reiterated, 'I am more patient than death, I am more patient than injustice,' and then walked out at the open door into the snow.

'I don't think she feels it, sir,' said the waiter, opening my door for me to enter.

I do not think she did. I watched her from my window. She took up a handful of the newly fallen snow and thrust it into her bosom, then hugged it close, as if it were a living thing, that could be warmed by that eager clasp; I saw also, as she turned her dark face up towards the sky, that the angry scowl left it. I should imagine that all sensation in her was dead, except in one corner of her heart, to which had gathered the memory of some miserable wrong, whose acuteness would bide with her to the day of her death.

Her name, as I learnt on further inquiry, was Hester. She had been born and bred in the Yorkshire dales; her parents were of the yeoman class, and poor through improvidence rather than misfortune. As a girl, Hester was remarkable for her pride and her beauty, of which no more relics remained than are left of the summer rose garden in drear and misty November. She received the scant education common to her condition half-a-century ago, and grew up a wild, wilful-tempered girl, impatient of all restraint, and eager for change and excitement. At sixteen she married, and very shortly afterwards her husband found it expedient to leave the dales, and to enlist in a regiment which was ordered on foreign service. Hester followed him to India, and led the life of camps for several years. During this interval her family lost sight of her completely; for, having parted in anger, no correspondence was kept up between them. This silence and separation lasted full nine years, during which time, Death dealt hardly with those left at home. Of all the large family of sons and daughters whom the old people had seen grow up to man's and woman's estate, not one survived. Their hearts began to soften towards the offending child, and they made efforts to learn if the regiment to which her husband belonged had returned to England. It had not.

One bleak and wintry night, while the solitary and bereaved couple were sitting by their silent hearth – it was a very lonely and retired spot where the house stood – a heavy step came up the little garden path. Neither of them stirred. They thought it was one of the farm servants returning from the village, whither he had been sent on some errand. The curtains had not been closed over the window, and all the room, filled with the shine of a yule-tide fire, was visible to the wayfarer without. The mother sat facing the window; lifting her slow, dull gaze from the white wood ashes on the hearth, she looked across towards it, and uttered a low, frightened cry. She saw a dark face peering in at the glass, which wore the traits of her daughter Hester. She thought it was her wraith,[54] and said so to the old man, who, taking a lantern, went out to see if anybody was lurking about. It was a very boisterous night: loud with wind, and black with clouds of sleety rain. At the threshold he stumbled over a dark form, which had crouched there for the slight shelter offered by the porch. He lowered the lantern, and threw the light on the face of a woman.

'Dame! dame! It is our bairn; it is like Hester!'

The mother appeared, and, with a great, gasping cry, recognised her daughter.

They led her into the house, towards the glowing heat of the fire, and set her down by the hearth; for her limbs would scarcely support her. Hester wore a thin and ragged cloak, beneath the folds of which she had hidden her child from the storm. He had fallen asleep in her bosom; but as her mother removed the dripping garment from her shoulders, he woke up with a laugh of childish surprise and pleasure. He was a fine, well-grown boy, of from six to seven years old, and showed none of those signs of want and suffering which had graven premature age upon the wasted features and gaunt frame of his mother. It was some time before Hester recovered from her frozen exhaustion, and then her first and eager demand was for food for the child.

'O Heaven, pity me!' cried the old woman, who was weeping over the pair, 'Hester and her lad starving, while there was to spare at home!'

She supplied their wants soon, and would have taken the boy; but Hester held him to her with a close and jealous grasp, chafing his limbs, warming his little hands in her bosom, and covering his hand with passionate kisses.

He fell asleep in her arms at last; and then she told her brief story. She was widowed; her husband had died in India from wound-fever, and she had been sent home to England; on her arrival there she found herself destitute, and had traversed the country on foot, subsisting by the casual charity of strangers. Thus much she said, and no more. She indulged in no details of her own exquisite sufferings; perhaps they were forgotten, when she ended by saying, 'Thank the Lord, the lad is saved!'

Hester lived on at the farm with her parents; and, as the old man failed more and more daily, she took the vigorous management of it upon herself, and things throve with them. By degrees, her beauty was restored, and then she had repeated offers of marriage; for, the inheritance which would be hers at her father's death was by no means despicable. But, she kept herself single, for the lad's sake. Wilfred grew strong, handsome, and high-spirited – like his mother, indeed, with whom, much as they loved each other, he had many a fierce contention. He never could bear to be thwarted or checked by her, and often Hester, in the bitterness of her unbridled anger, would cry, 'O Wilfred! it would have been better for thee and thy mother if we had died on the door-stone in the snow, that night we came home.'

Still, she had an intense pride in him; and always, after their quarrels, she allowed his extravagance to have freer scope, though that was what usually led to their disputes. As might have been expected, Wilfred, under such uncertain training, became reckless, wild, and domineering, though he preserved a certain rough generosity and frankness of character which redeemed his faults, and made him a favourite with the country folks, and a sort of king amongst his companions, whose superior in all rustic sports he was.

His grandfather died when he was nineteen; his grandmother, eighteen months later. Then Hester was sole mistress of the little farm. Wilfred soon began to urge his mother to sell the property and leave the dales, whose uneventful quiet fretted his restless disposition. This she absolutely refused to do; and was on one occasion so deeply irritated at his persistence as to say:

'I would sell the Ings to save your life, Wilfred, but for nothing less!'

There was at this time, living on a neighboring farm, an old man of the name of Price, who had a granddaughter to keep his house. She was called Nelly; and, besides being a small heiress, was a beauty, and something of a coquette. Nelly had a short, plump little figure; a complexion as soft and clear as a blush-rose, and auburn hair. Wilfred fell in love. He was a tall, hardy, self-willed, and proud young fellow; but in Nelly's hands he was plastic as wax, and weak as water. She encouraged him, teased him, caressed him, mocked him, set him beside himself. She played off all her little witcheries and fascinations upon him; looked sweetly unconscious of their mischievous influence; and, when Wilfred stormed, and raved, she laughed in his face. He wanted to marry her immediately; she had played with him long enough, he thought; and one evening when she had been soft and coy, rather than teasing, he put his fortune to the proof. She told him flatly she did not like him – wherein Nelly told anything but the truth, as perhaps better women have done under like circumstances.

Wilfred took her reply in earnest, and went away in a rage – mad, jealous, and burning with passionate disappointment. Hester hated Nelly, and gave her not a few hard words; for in her camp life, the mother had called some epithets, more expressive than polite, which she used with vigorous truth when her wrath was excited. She kept her son's wound raw and sore by frequent scornful allusions to his 'Nelly Graceless,' and did her best to widen the breach between them with ample success.

Wilfred stayed away from the Prices for ten whole days.

This desertion did not suit the golden-headed but tinsel-hearted little coquette. She contrived to meet him in a shady woodwalk, where they had often loitered together. He was out with his dog and gun; very ill at ease in mind, for his handsome face looked sullen and dangerous, and he would not see her as she passed by. Mortified and angry, Nelly went home and cried herself ill. Wilfred heard she had caught a fever, and must needs go to ask. She met him at the garden gate, with a smile and a blush; whereat Wilfred was so glad, that he forgot to reproach her. There was, in consequence, a complete reconciliation, ratified by kisses and promises – light coin with beauty Nell, but real heart-gold with poor, infatuated Wilfred. Hester almost despised her son when she heard of it.

'She is only fooling thee, lad!' said she, indignantly. 'Come a richer suitor to the door, she'll throw thee over. She is only a light, false-hearted lass, not worth a whistle of thine.'

Therein Hester spake truth.

Nelly played with her lover as a cat plays with a mouse. Wilfred urged their marriage. She would one day, and the next day she would not. Then arose other difficulties. Hester did not want an interloper by her fireside, and would not give up the farm to her son; in fact, she was so jealous of his affection, that the thought of his marriage was hateful to her. Old Price said the young folks might settle with him, if they would; but Nelly liked the house at the Ings bettter, and thought Wilfred ought to take her there. When he explained that the property was his mother's for her life, she immediately accused him of not loving her, and assumed a decided coldness and repulsiveness of manner. Wilfred, both hurt and angry, tried to give her up, but his bonds were not so easily escaped. If he stayed away from her two days, on the third he was sure to be at her side, either winning her with tender words, or reproaching her with bitter ones. Nelly must have found the game a pleasant one, for she kept it up a long time, undergoing herself as many changes of hue and form as a bubble blown up into the sunshine.

Frequently, during his lengthy visits at the Glebe Farm, Wilfred had encountered a man, Joseph Rigby by name, a dales yeoman, and one of considerable wealth, but no education. This man was one of the last in the world to excite jealousy; but presently Wilfred was compelled to see that Nelly gave the coarse-mannered, middle-aged Rigby, more of her attentions than consorted with her position as his promised wife. He charged her with the fact. At first she denied it with blushes, and tears, and loud protestations; but at last confessed that Rigby had proposed to her – she did not dare to add that she had half accepted him. They parted in mutual displeasure; and old Price said as they agreed so badly, they had better break off the match, and Nelly should marry Joseph Rigby, who was well-to-do, and would know how to keep his wife in order. Wilfred went near her no more. Presently, it was rumoured in the countryside that Nelly Price and Mr Rigby were to be married after the October fairs. Hester sneered, prophesied that the rich yeoman would repent his bargain before St Mark's, and rejoiced greatly at her son's escape.

Meanwhile, Wilfred went about the farm and the house, silent, moody, and spiritless. He was quite changed, and, as his mother thought, for the better. Instead of associating with his former companions, he stayed much at home, and again renewed his entreaties that his mother would sell the Ings, and leave the dales altogether. He wanted to emigrate. He did not care where they went, so that they got away from that hateful place. Hester was as reluctant as ever to comply; but she modified her refusal – they would try a year longer: if he were still in the same mind at the end of that period – well, perhaps she would yield to his urgent wishes.

On the morning of the Leeford Fair he left home early, and returned towards dusk – so it was said by Hester. No other person saw him until noon next day. Joseph Rigby was found murdered, and thrown into a gully by the Leeford road, that night. There were traces of a violent struggle upon the road, and the body had been dragged some distance. It had been rifled of money and watch, but a broad engraved ring which Rigby wore on the fourth finger of his left hand, was not removed. He was known to have left the market ball at Leeford with a considerable sum in gold upon his person, for his brother-in-law had remonstrated with him about carrying so much; but the doomed man made light of his warnings. The whole country-side was up, for the murder was a barbarous one. Suspicion fell at once on Hester's son. His behaviour at Leeford had attracted observation. He.had been seen to use angry gestures to Rigby, who had laughed at him, and had offered the young man his hand, as if wishing to be friends; the other had rejected it, and turned away, shaking his clenched fist. He had also been seen to mount his horse at the inn-door, and ride off in the afternoon. Rigby started about an hour later, and alone. He was seen no more until his body was found in the ditch by some men going to their work in the morning.

When Wilfred was taken, he and his mother were sitting by the fireside together; she sewing; he reading. It was towards twilight, and he had not been over the threshold all day. He was very downcast and gloomy; irritable when spoken to, and short in his answers. His mother said to him that he was very strange, and added that she wished he would give over hankering after Nelly Graceless. He laughed painfully, and did not lift his eyes from his book. There was a loud knock at the door. Hester rose and opened it. Three men pushed their way into the house, the foremost asking if her son was at home.

'Yes; he is in there, by the fire. What do you want with him?'

'You must come with us, Mr Wilfred – nay, it's no use showing fight,' cried a burly, muscular fellow, laying his hand heavily on his shoulder; for Wilfred had turned deadly pale, and had attempted to shake off the man's grasp.

'What is it for?' asked Hester, with her eyes on her son.

'God knows. – I don't,' said he, quietly.

'Mr Rigby was robbed and murdered last night, as he came home from Leeford Fair, and suspicion points at your lad, mistress,' said the man, who still held his hand on Wilfred's shoulder.

Hester gave utterance to no frantic denials; she laughed, even.

'Why he was at home by this hour yesterday, in this very room, at his tea. Wasn't he, Jessy?' said she, turning to the maidservant; who, with a countenance of alarm, stood by the door.

The girl said 'Yes;' then hesitated, and added that she didn't see young master when she brought in tea.

'I was upstairs,' said Wilfred.

'You had better keep all that for another time and place: you must go with us now,' observed the man.

Wilfred made no resistance. His mother brought him his coat, and helped him to put it on.

'Say thou didn't do it, Willy – only say so?' whispered she, fiercely.

'I didn't mother: so help me God!' was his fervent reply.

'You hear him!' cried Hester, turning to the men; 'you hear him! He never lied in his days. He might have killed Rigby in a fair fight, or in hot blood; but he is not the lad to lie in wait at night, to murder his enemy and rob him! He is not a thief, this son of mine!'

The officers urged their departure. Wilfred was placed in the vehicle which had been brought for the purpose, and driven off.

'I'll follow thee, Willy!' cried his mother. 'Keep up thy heart; they can't touch thee! Good-bye, my poor lad!'

They were out of hearing, and Hester turned back into the house, cursing Nelly Graceless in her heart.

Wilfred was committed to take his trial at the winter gaol-delivery on a charge of wilful murder. The evidence against him was overwhelming. Hester sold the Ings and collected all the money she could, that, if gold would buy his redemption, it might be done; for herself, she had a perfect faith in his innocence, and was confident of his acquittal, but few persons, if any, shared her feelings. The best legal advice had been retained for the accused, and the trial came on shortly before Christmas. Hester was the only witness for her son. The woman Jessy's evidence damaged his cause considerably. She contradicted herself over and over again, and at last, flurried and confused, she burst into tears, crying out that she would say anything to get her young master off. There was nobody to speak with certainty as to the prisoner's having been at home by a certain hour but his mother; he had put his horse into the stable himself, the groom being absent at the fair, and Jessy could not swear that he was in to tea; she believed not; only one cup was used.

Two witnesses, labourers on a farm near the Ings, swore to having seen and spoken to the prisoner after the hour stated; they said he was riding fast, and seemed agitated, but it was too dark to see his face. Nelly Price also had her word against him; it was drawn from her reluctantly, in the midst of shame-faced tears and noisy sobs, but it quite overthrew the attempt to prove an alibi. She stated that she had watched until dark, in the garden, for Wilfred's return from Leeford, and had not seen him go by. The prisoner never looked towards her, but murmured that he had gone home by the bridle-road and Low Lane to avoid passing the Glebe Farm. The former witnesses, on being recalled, said that it was on the highway, nearly a mile from the place where the lower road branched off, and nearer to the Ings, that they encountered the accused. These two decent men, being strictly cross-examined, never swerved from their first story an iota, and agreed in every particular. They were individuals of decent character; both had worked on the prisoner's farm, and acknowledged him to be a liberal and kind master. Their evidence was not to be shaken. As a final and damning proof of guilt, the watch of which the murdered man had been robbed was produced; it had been found concealed under the thatch of an out-house at the Ings. At this point of the evidence the prisoner was observed to draw himself up and look round defiantly, –

despair gave him a fictitious strength, perhaps, or, was it conscious innocence!

Wilfred spoke in his own defence, briefly, but strongly. His life, he said, was sworn away, but he was as guiltless of the crime laid to his charge as any of those gentlemen who sat in judgment upon him. His mother, who had remained in court all the time and had never spoken except when called upon for her evidence, had preserved a stoical calmness throughout. When he ceased to speak however, she cried out in a quivering voice:

'My lad, thy mother believes thee!'

Some friend would have led her out, but she refused to go. The jury gave their verdict of guilty without any recommendation to mercy, and the sentence of death was pronounced. Then it was that Hester rose on her feet and faltered that formula of words with which she had startled me in the corridor:

'He is not guilty, my lord judge. God will right him yet. It will all come out some day. I can wait; yes, I can wait. I am more patient than death. I am more patient than injustice.'

Wilfred died stubborn and unconfessing; on the scaffold, with his last breath, he persisted in asserting his innocence. His mother bade him farewell, and was carried to this inn, where she had stayed, raving in a frenzy-fit. For many months she was subject to restraint, but, recovering in some measure, she was at length set at liberty. Her mind was still distraught, however; she wandered back to the dales and to her old home, but the new owner had taken possession, and after enduring her intrusions for some time, he was compelled to apply for her removal.

After this, her money being lost or exhausted, she strayed about the country in a purposeless way; begging or doing day's work in the field, until she strayed here again, and became the Pensioner of the Holly-Tree. The poor demented creature is always treated kindly, but her son's sentence has not yet been reversed in men's judgment. Every morning during the time the judges are in the neighbouring Assize town[55] she waits in one of the streets through which they must pass to reach the court; and as the gilt coach, the noisy trumpets, and the decrepit halberdiers[56] go by, she scowls at them from beneath her shaggy brows, and mutters her formula of defiance. She will die saying it: comforting her poor, worn, wounded heart with its smarting balm.

Will she find, when she comes before the Tribunal of Eternal Decrees, that she has leaned thus long on a broken reed, or will she find her son there, free from the guilt of blood?

The Great Judge only knows.

THE BILL
[by Charles Dickens]

I could scarcely believe, when I came to the last word of the foregoing recital and finished it off with a flourish, as I am apt to do when I make an end of any writing, that I had been snowed up a whole week. The time had hung so lightly on my hands, and the Holly-Tree, so bare at first, had born so many berries for me, that I should have been in great doubt of the fact but for a piece of documentary evidence that lay upon my table.

The road had been dug out of the snow, on the previous day, and the document in question was my Bill. It testified, emphatically, to my having eaten and drunk, and warmed myself, and slept, among the sheltering branches of the Holly-Tree, seven days and nights.

I had yesterday allowed the road twenty-four hours to improve itself, finding that I required that additional margin of time for the completion of my task. I had ordered my Bill to be upon the table, and a chaise to be at the door, 'at eight o'clock tomorrow evening.' It was eight o'clock tomorrow evening, when I buckled up my travelling writing desk in its leather case, paid my Bill, and got on my warm coats and wrappers. Of course, no time now remained for my travelling on, to add a frozen tear to the icicles which were doubtless hanging plentifully about the farmhouse where I had first seen Angela. What I had to do, was, to get across to Liverpool by the shortest open road, there to meet my heavy baggage and embark. It was quite enough to do, and I had not an hour too much time to do it in.

I had taken leave of all my Holly-Tree friends – almost, for the time being, of my bashfulness too – and was standing for half a minute at the Inn-door, watching the ostler as he took another turn at the cord which tied my portmanteau on the chaise, when I saw lamps coming down towards the Holly-Tree. The road was so padded with snow that no wheels were audible; but, all of us who were standing at the Inn-door, saw lamps coming on, and at a lively rate too, between the walls of snow that had been heaped up, on either side of the track. The chambermaid instantly divined how the case stood, and called to the ostler; 'Tom, this is a Gretna job!' The ostler, knowing that her sex instinctively scented a marriage or anything in that direction, rushed up the yard, bawling, 'Next four out!' and in a moment the whole establishment was thrown into commotion.

I had a melancholy interest in seeing the happy man who loved and was beloved; and, therefore, instead of driving off at once, I remained at the Inn-door when the fugitives drove up. A bright-eyed fellow, muffled in a mantle, jumped out so briskly that he almost overthrew me. He turned to apologise, and, by Heaven, it was Edwin!

'Charley!' said he, recoiling. 'Gracious powers, what do you do here?'

'Edwin,' said I, recoiling, 'Gracious powers, what do *you* do here!' I struck my forehead as I said it, and an insupportable blaze of light seemed to shoot before my eyes.

He hurried me into the little parlour (always kept with a slow fire in it and no poker), where posting company waited while their horses were putting to; and shutting the door, said:

'Charley, forgive me!'

'Edwin!' I returned. 'Was this well? When I loved her so dearly! When I had garnered up my heart so long!' I could say no more.

He was shocked when he saw how moved I was, and made the cruel observation, that he had not thought I should have taken it so much to heart.

I looked at him. I reproached him no more. But I looked at him.

'My dear, dear Charley,' said he; 'don't think ill of me, I beseech you! I know you have a right to my utmost confidence, and believe me, you have ever had it until now. I abhor secresy. Its meanness is intolerable to me. But I and my dear girl have observed it for your sake.'

He and his dear girl! It steeled me.

'You have observed it for my sake, sir?' said I, wondering how his frank face could face it out so.

'Yes! – and Angela's,' said he.

I found the room reeling round in an uncertain way, like a labouring humming-top. 'Explain yourself,' said I, holding on by one hand to an armchair.

'Dear old darling Charley!' returned Edwin, in his cordial manner, 'Consider! When you were going on so happily with Angela, why should I compromise you with the old gentleman by making you a party to our engagement, and (after he had declined my proposals) to our secret intention? Surely it was better that you should be able honorably to say, "He never took counsel with me, never told me, never breathed a word of it." If Angela suspected it and showed me all the favor and support she could – God bless her for a precious creature and a priceless wife! – I couldn't help that. Neither I nor Emmeline ever told her, any more than we told you. And for the same good reason, Charley; trust me, for the same good reason, and no other upon earth!'

Emmeline was Angela's cousin. Lived with her. Had been brought up with her. Was her father's ward. Had property.

'Emmeline is in the chaise, dear Edwin?' said I, embracing him with the greatest affection.

'My good fellow!' said he, 'Do you suppose I should be going to Gretna Green without her!'

I ran out with Edwin, I opened the chaise door, I took Emmeline in my arms, I folded her to my heart. She was wrapped in soft white fur, like the snowy landscape; but was warm, and young, and lovely. I put their leaders to with my own hands, I gave the boys a five-pound note apiece, I cheered them as they drove away, I drove the other way myself as hard as I could pelt.

I never went to Liverpool, I never went to America, I went straight back to London, and I married Angela. I have never until this time, even to her, disclosed the secret of my character, and the mistrust and mistaken journey into which it led me. When she, and they, and our eight children and their seven – I mean Edwin's and Emmeline's, whose eldest girl is old enough now to wear white fur herself, and to look very like her mother in it – come to read these pages, as of course they will, I shall hardly fail to be found out at last. Never mind! I can bear it. I began at the Holly-Tree, by idle accident, to associate the Christmas time of year with human interest, and with some inquiry into, and some care for, the lives of those by whom I find myself surrounded. I hope that I am none the worse for it, and that no one near me or afar off is the worse for it. And I say, May the green Holly-Tree flourish, striking its roots deep into our English ground, and having its germinating qualities carried by the birds of Heaven all over the world!

NOTES

1. Inns of court between the Thames and Fleet Street, possessed in the thirteenth century by the Knights Templar.

2. Public-houses are taverns, usually attached to inns, providing refreshment and/or entertainments for community members and travellers; a rime is a frozen fog or mist.

3. The earliest northbound railways from London opened in 1838 and 1844 from Euston Square, followed by the Great Northern Railway from King's Cross in 1846.

4. The open-air seat outside a coach, called a 'box' seat because its location is atop a covered chest, or box, built into the front of the vehicle and frequently providing a seat for the driver.

5. Especially for northbound vehicles carrying passengers, mail, or goods out of London, the renowned Peacock Inn, dating from 1564, served as a point of departure. Purl is warm beer infused with gin and spices or herbs, usually ginger and sugar; also called 'dog's nose'.

6. An 1813 bridge across north London's Hornsey Lane.

7. Robert Burns' 1788 poem relating a traditional Scottish folk song, the title of which translates literally as 'old long-since'. Soon after its publication, singing the song at the New Year became customary, and the narrator's invocation of it here suggests its repetition as an irritant.

8. The primary northbound road out of London, now the A1 road.

9. Not to be confused with 'japanned' objects covered entirely in black lacquer, folding japanned screens featured calligraphy and elaborate, decorative scene painting.

10. Founded by German physiologist Franz Joseph Gall (1758–1828), phrenology claimed to map mental prowess using the shape of one's cranium and was popular, despite vocal sceptics, in the nineteenth century. Wilkie Collins, Dickens' friend and a contributor to this number, had a notably large cranial bump on his forehead.

11. A notorious village in southern Scotland where couples eloped due to more permissive Scottish marriage laws.

12. The Song-book is likely *The Songster Miscellany, or Vocal Companion; to which are added Toasts and Sentiments* (1800). The Jest-book possibly refers to *Death's Jest-Book; or, The Fool's Tragedy* (1850), a dramatic work in five acts published rather ironically after its author, the poet Thomas Lovell Beddoes (1803–49), had committed suicide. *The Adventures of Peregrine Pickle* is Tobias Smollett's (1721–71) picaresque 1751 novel, and *A Sentimental Journey through France and Italy, by Mr Yorick* (1768) is Laurence Sterne's (1713–68) humourous autobiographical travel narrative.

13. The story of Raymond and Agnes is a sub-plot in Matthew Gregory Lewis' (1775–1818) path-breaking Gothic novel *The Monk* (1796), and theatrical adaptations

of the story, such as one staged in 1809, emphasised the attention-grabbing quality of the story of 'The Bleeding Nun of the Castle of Lindenberg'.

14. This account accurately relates the highlights of the case of Mr Jonathan Bradford, an Oxford innkeeper unjustly executed for murder in 1742, excepting the information about the servant's position. Mr Christopher Hayes, the guest beside whose body Mr Bradford was found holding a knife, was actually murdered by his own footman (not the ostler) before Mr Bradford could follow through with his own plan of murdering and robbing the man. The footman confessed on his own deathbed years after Mr Bradford had been executed, and the story was adapted for the stage in *Jonathan Bradford,* an 1835 drama by Edward Fitzball.

15. Another reference to Lewis' *The Monk* (1796), which includes the ballad of Alonzo and Imogene. When Alonzo goes to war, Imogene promises that she will never marry another, even if Alonzo dies. They agree that, should she violate this vow, Alonzo's ghost will spoil the wedding celebrations by carrying her to her death. Imogene marries another, and Alonzo's ghost arrives to fulfil his promise, as described in lines 56–60 of the ballad: 'The worms they crept in, and the worms they crept out, / And sported his locks and his temples about / As the spectre addressed Imogene.'

16. Dickens combines two actual locations here: The Mitre Inn is in Chatham, where Dickens lived as a small child, and the 'cathedral town' suggests nearby Rochester.

17. A reference to 'The Story of Prince Ahmed and the Peri Banou' in *The Arabian Nights,* also known as *One Thousand and One Nights,* a popular collection of Arabic tales dating from the eighth century and one of Dickens' favourite books. In this tale, Prince Husayn and his younger brothers, Ali and Ahmed, compete on separate quests to find the most magnificent treasure, which will earn its owner the hand of Nour Al-Nihar, their beautiful cousin. Husayn finds a piece of enchanted carpet enabling its riders to fly, but Ali ultimately wins Nour Al-Nihar's hand. Later in the tale, the Princess Peri Banou, a fairy, becomes Ahmed's love interest.

18. Dickens himself stayed at an inn in Wiltshire in 1848, and editors have speculated that his narrator here refers to the Salisbury Inn, Winterslow Hut (now the Peacock Inn), or the White Hart Inn. In the early- to mid-nineteenth century, bitter, or pale ale, began to replace the heavier and darker porter as Britain's most prominent beer.

19. Since at least the sixteenth century, literary texts reference the legend that one cannot precisely count the stones of Stonehenge. Similar legends circulate about many such megalithic sites, including the Rollright Stones on the Oxfordshire/ Warwickshire border, and Little Kit's Coty, also known as 'The Countless Stones', in Kent.

20. The bustard bird disappeared from Britain by the late 1830s, and the dodo bird had been extinct since the late seventeenth century. The great bustard, known for its large size, long legs, and speed, survived in other lands and was reintroduced to Salisbury Plain, its previous habitat in Britain, in the year 2004.

21. Metempsychosis is the movement of the soul from a deceased body into a living body; in some religions, the two bodies need not be of the same species. The Athanasian Creed is named for Athanasius (c. 298–373), its probable author and a defender of the Trinity. The creed is a statement of Christian principles endorsed by the Catholic as well as the Anglican Churches.

22. Shedding or sloughing; in the case of birds, the feather loss that enables a change of plumage.

23. A mixture of opium dissolved in alcohol, laudanum was easily purchased in small doses to treat a wide range of complaints, including chronic pain, sleep disorders, or fussy infants. Taken in large doses, the drug was lethal.

24. 'White bears' may be a misprint for 'white beards'. Alternatively, the reference to 'humbugs', indicating fraud or a hoax, suggests the costuming of other animals as white bears, which do not exist in Wales.

25. Bannocks are round, unleavened bread cakes, sometimes containing fruit; Athol brose is oatmeal with whisky and honey.

26. A small island in a river.

27. The villain of a fairy tale recorded in Charles Perrault's (1628–1703) *Histoires ou Contes du temps passé* (1697), translated into English by Robert Samber and sold as *Histories or Tales of Times Past* in 1729. Bluebeard tells his new bride that she may go anywhere except into his secret Blue Chamber, where he secretly stores the corpses of his dead wives. When Bluebeard discovers that his new wife has entered the chamber, his attempt to murder her is thwarted by her brothers' arrival.

28. A tocsin is an alarm bell; the Biblical story of the Tower of Babel, which reached to heaven, records it as such a remarkable example of communal human achievement that the Lord decided he must 'confound their language, that they may not understand one another's speech' (Genesis 11: 7).

29. Cobbler may be a shortened reference to or a chilled version of 'cobbler's punch', a warm drink usually consisting of beer, ale, wine, or gin in addition to sugar and spices. Juleps, slings, and cocktails are all sweetened spirit drinks with American origins that have various fruit flavourings; juleps most often contain mint.

30. Biblical allusion to the Book of Matthew, in which Jesus preaches to the multitudes: 'And why beholdest thou the mote that is in thy brother's eye, but considerest not the beam that is in thine own eye? / Or how wilt thou say to thy brother, Let me pull out the mote out of thine eye; and, behold, a beam [is] in thine own eye? / Thou hypocrite, first cast out the beam out of thine own eye; and then shalt thou see clearly to cast out the mote out of thy brother's eye' (Matthew 7: 3–5).

31. Imprisoned for a total of sixteen years by Frederick the Great (1712–86), Friedrich von der Trenck (1726–94) was a Prussian soldier whose exaggerated sufferings reached a wide European audience via the three-volume memoir: *Des Freiherrn von der Trenck merkwürdige Lebensgeschichte* (1787).

32. The infamous Bastille in Paris housed prisoners without trial at the behest of

noblemen or royalty and was triumphantly stormed by Revolutionaries on
14th July 1879. Dickens' description of a traumatised prisoner whose spirit is broken
by long-term confinement looks forward to the character of Dr Alexandre Manette
in *A Tale of Two Cities* (1859).

33. An ironic invocation of the famous quote attributed to the Roman ruler Julius
Caesar (100–44 BCE): 'I came. I saw. I conquered.' (*Veni. Vidi. Vici.* in Latin.)

34. 'Family' appears to be a misprint for 'faculty'; in later printings of this story,
Wilkie Collins corrected the error.

35. A weak and inexpensively made candle consisting of a stalk from a rush plant
dipped in grease or tallow.

36. In John Home's (1722–1808) tragedy *Douglas* (1756), the orphaned Norval is
raised by a shepherd. Nineteenth-century ballads based on the romantic tragedy
often began with the following lines: 'My name is Norval; on the Grampian hills /
My father feeds his flocks; a frugal swain,'Whose constant cares were to increase
his store.' 'The Young May Moon' and 'When He Who Adores Thee' are songs
from *Irish Melodies* (1808–34) by Thomas Moore (1779–1852), a popular early
nineteenth-century poet.

37. Originally printed as 'kings's'.

38. Originally at the White Hart Inn in Ware, England, this enormous bed was
constructed around the year 1590 and became an immediate tourist attraction. The
four-posted covered bed is surrounded by curtains and measures 3.25 metres square,
equalling the size of beds made for royalty.

39. A flat cake made of baked apple.

40. Dickens, perhaps unintentionally, inverts the morality of the legend. To win the
Trojan War, the Greeks were dishonest in presenting a giant horse to the Trojans that
was filled with warriors rather than the promised good luck.

41. The word 'hard' was originally printed, probably in error, as 'heard'.

42. Making its first appearance in London in 1829, the omnibus was a large horse-
drawn vehicle in which passengers sat upon facing benches as they travelled along
a fixed route.

43. The Christmas tree became popular in Britain after Prince Albert (1819–61), of
German heritage, introduced one to Windsor Castle in 1841. Also from the German,
Christkind means 'Christ Child'; in the nineteenth century, this angelic, child-like
figure brought holiday presents in Germany and some other parts of western
Europe. Costumed women often played the role of the Christkindchen in Christmas
Eve festivities.

44. *Narrative of a Residence in South Africa* (1834), written by the Scottish poet
Thomas Pringle (1789–1834), who lived in South Africa briefly and also published
Some Account of the present state of the English Settlers in Albany, South Africa (1824)
and *Ephemerides; or occasional poems. Written in Scotland and South Africa* (1828).
Daniel Defoe's *Robinson Crusoe* was first published in 1719.

45. Mr Tattenhall's expression refers to the notion that toads and other amphibians can survive for shockingly long periods of time in enclosed spaces that would seem fatal. Breaking even financially rather than turning a profit is as frustrating to Mr Tattenhall as being trapped in a wall.

46. Also called blackthorn tree, which leaves behind sloe.

47. Raincoats were known as mackintoshes, after the Glaswegian company founded by Scotsman Charles Macintosh (1766–1843), who in 1823 patented the first method of waterproofing cloth.

48. Lord John Russell (1792–1878), Colonial Secretary in 1843, the year referenced in this story, and later Prime Minister (1846–52, 1865–66), instituted the Crown Lands Sale Act in 1842, which set the minimum price for an acre of land at one pound.

49. Psalm 23:4 'Yea, though I walk through the valley of the shadow of death, I will fear no evil: for thou [art] with me; thy rod and thy staff they comfort me.'

50. Dark, usually column-shaped, rocks produced as a result of fire.

51. Eucalyptus trees.

52. The bough of an Acacia tree, called a wattle-tree in Australia.

53. Covered with pinkish purple flowers even on its trunk, *Cercis Siliquastrum* is a tree indigenous to western Asia and the Mediterranean that has been grown in Britain since the 1500s. Its name suggests the belief that Judas Iscariot hanged himself from such a tree.

54. The apparition of a dead person or the spectre of a living person whose death is, consequently, presumed to be imminent.

55. The assizes were criminal or civil court proceedings presided over by superior court judges who determined sentences after seated juries decided the merits of cases. The periodic sessions held in each county of England allowed for the routine administration of justice across the land while minimising travel for the litigants of each case.

56. Soldiers or ceremonial officers carrying halberds, long-handled weapons that combine the features of a battle-axe with a spear.

BIOGRAPHICAL NOTE

Charles Dickens (1812–70), a true celebrity in the Victorian period, remains one of the best-known British writers. His most popular works, such as *Great Expectations* (1861) and *A Christmas Carol* (1843), continue to be read and adapted worldwide. In addition to fourteen complete novels, Dickens wrote short stories, essays, and plays. He acted on the stage more than once in amateur theatricals of his own production, and at the end of his life gave a series of powerful public readings from his works. Dickens' journalism is a lesser-known yet central aspect of his life and career. In 1850, he founded *Household Words*, where he worked as editor in chief in addition to writing over one hundred pieces himself. After over twenty years of marriage, in 1858, Dickens abruptly separated from his wife Catherine in order to pursue a relationship with Ellen Ternan, a young actress. A dispute with his publishers, one of whom was representing Catherine in the separation negotiations, caused Dickens to engage in court proceedings over the rights to the name *Household Words*. As a result of winning the suit, Dickens folded *Household Words* into a new journal, *All the Year Round*, in 1859, with an increased focus on serialised fiction. From 1850 until 1867, Dickens published a special issue of these journals each December that he called the Christmas number. Collaborative in nature, including the work of up to nine different authors, the Christmas numbers were extremely popular and frequently imitated by other publishers. *The Holly-Tree Inn* is a charming example of what would become one of Dickens' most profitable endeavours, for the Christmas numbers often sold over 200,000 copies.

Wilkie Collins (1824–89) was an innovator in the genres of detective and sensation fiction as well as one of Dickens' closest companions and collaborators. He published some of his most successful novels, including the phenomenally popular *The Woman in White* (1860) and *The Moonstone* (1868), in *All the Year Round* and sometimes managed the journal in Dickens' absence. Collins and Dickens also collaborated on multiple theatrical productions, including *The Frozen Deep* (1857). Three Christmas numbers – *The Wreck of the Golden Mary* (1856), *The Perils of Certain English Prisoners* (1857), and *No Thoroughfare* (1867) – contain only the work of Dickens and Collins, and *No Thoroughfare* was also a successful stage production. In addition to his work as a novelist and playwright, Collins found success as a journalist for several periodicals and wrote a well-received travel book, *Rambles Beyond Railways* (1851). Collins' best-known work, *The Moonstone*, is one of the first detective novels in English and remains one of the most impressive examples of the form. His fiction often challenges nineteenth-century social convention, giving voice to characters with physical disabilities and advocating a subversion of many sexual norms. In Collins' personal life, he raised children with two women simultaneously, maintaining each in her own household and consistently opposing the institution of marriage.

William Howitt (1792–1879) was an ardent advocate of social reform who wrote poetry and prose. He regularly published journalism on political as well as general topics, sometimes using the pseudonym Wilfred Wender early in his career, and in the late 1830s he began a series of successful books treating the English countryside: *The Rural Life of England* (1838), *The Boy's Country-Book* (1839), and *Visits to*

Remarkable Places (1840). Howitt was an important figure in the early career of Elizabeth Gaskell, who placed pieces in his short-lived *Howitt's Journal*, established in May 1847 before Howitt faced bankruptcy the following year. Married in 1821, William and his wife Mary lived for a short time in Germany, and the two collaborated on *The Forest Minstrel, and Other Poems* (1823), *The Literature and Romance of Northern Europe* (1852), and other works. United in support of social reform, Dickens asked both William and Mary Howitt to contribute to *Household Words* in its early years, and William contributed pieces such as 'The Queen's Tobacco Pipe' (4th January 1851) and 'Two Days in Rio Janeiro' (4th August 1855). Howitt was raised a Quaker, then later became a radical Unitarian and spiritualist; his friendship with Dickens ruptured because Dickens disagreed with Howitt's strong belief in spiritualism. In 1852, Howitt travelled to Australia where he joined the searched for gold, an experience that clearly influenced his story for this Christmas number as well as a number of books that followed, including *Land, Labour, and Gold, or, Two Years in Victoria* (1855). Howitt's works include multiple editions of *Homes and Haunts of the Most Eminent British Poets* (1847), and he contributed to the very popular *Cassell's Illustrated History of England* (1856–64). In their final years, the Howitts struggled to cope with the fact that two of their children had died, and they spent much of their time in Rome, where William is buried.

Adelaide Anne Procter (1825–64) was a poet whose work earned admiration throughout Victorian society, from labourers to the middle classes to Queen Victoria. Procter was raised in a literary family, and her education at home and at Queen's College prepared her well for a life of letters. Because her father,

Bryan Waller Procter (1787–1874), was friends with influential figures, such as William Makepeace Thackeray, Thomas Carlyle, and Dickens, Procter originally submitted her poetry to Dickens using the pseudonym Mary Berwick. She withheld her true identity from Dickens for over a year, and Dickens reflected on his own surprise in an introduction he penned for an 1866 edition of Procter's most famous verse collection, *Legends and Lyrics* (1858–61). In addition to frequently contributing verse to *Household Words*, Procter published in *The Cornhill* and was active in the Langham Place Circle, a group of progressive women activists. She cultivated close relationships with some leading feminist figures of the day, including Matilda Hays (1820–97) and the American actress Charlotte Cushman (1816–76), who lived in what was then termed a 'female marriage'. Procter agitated for education and employment equity for girls and women, founding the Society for the Promotion of the Employment of Women (SPEW) in 1859 with Jessie Boucherett (1825–1905). Before a protracted battle with tuberculosis ended her life, Procter completed *A Chaplet of Verses* (1862), which she published to assist a refuge for homeless women and children.

Harriet Parr (1828–1900) left governessing for a literary career and first published using the pseudonym Holme Lee. When Dickens asked her to submit pieces to *Household Words*, he apparently did not realise that she had already placed her work in the journal under the pseudonym. Dickens admired Parr's second novel, *Gilbert Massenger* (1855), on the unsettling subject of hereditary insanity but, using its long length as a convenient excuse, did not accept it for publication in *Household Words* for fear of upsetting readers who might feel anxiety about the topic. *Gilbert Massenger* was promptly translated into French and Italian, and Parr's successive novels were consistently popular enough to prevent her from needing to return to work as a governess. In addition to over thirty novels, including *Against the Wind and Tide* (1859), *The Vicissitudes of Bessy Fairfax* (1874), and *Ben Wilmer's Wooing* (1876), Parr wrote non-fiction essays and historical works, such as *The Life and Death of Jeanne d'Arc* (1866). Harriet Parr died on the Isle of Wight, where she had happily resided for several decades.

Melisa Klimaszewski is an Assistant Professor at Drake University, where she specialises in Victorian literature, South African literature, and critical gender studies. She has published articles on nineteenth-century domestic servants and wet nurses, and is now pursuing a longer project that focuses on Victorian collaboration. Author of the forthcoming Hesperus title *Brief Lives: Wilkie Collins*, she has edited several of Dickens' collaborative Christmas numbers for Hesperus and is co-author of *Brief Lives: Charles Dickens* (2007).